LINES—

By

Geralyn Hesslau Magrady

COPYRIGHT

LINES—

by Geralyn Hesslau Magrady

Copyright © 2015 by Geralyn Hesslau Magrady

ISBN: 9781515141273

This story is inspired by actual historical events, but the characters, characterizations, actions, events, and locations depicted herein are either products of the author's imagination or are used fictitiously. Any resemblance to real persons, living or dead, is either coincidental or entirely for dramatic purposes, and is not intended as a reflection upon any actual person or historical occurrence.

Dedicated

to Mom and Dad—

for everything

Lines —

We're holding still our thoughts on faith,
and biting tongues for chief estates,
denying selves of destined mates—
Will these straight lines create our fate?

Some drawn, some veiled, but all's at stake
when those we sever make us ache,
when those we heed suppress our sake—
Which lines prevent our souls to wake?

Demanding truths to be exposed,
we'll risk the cuts by men opposed—
Will we then live our passion's prose?
Without the crossing, no one knows.

PREFACE

Dear Livia,

How goes the writing? Have you penned any lines worthy of Whitman or Collins? A couple of years down the line I expect to read your masterpiece, so I can brag about you, the sister with whom I spun tales in a cozy little loft. (You have no idea how I now appreciate that cramped space. This short time at Fort Kearny has given me much gratitude for that roof over our heads!)

I wish I could tell you this experience has fulfilled my dream, but that, of course, would not be the case. I do not initiate controversial conversation, but unfortunately, I was dragged into one and believe I ruffled a few feathers rather than gained any respect. I'm adamant about denying manifest destiny no matter my superiors' opinions, but I don't plan on foisting my ideals on others just yet, at least not while I'm still perceived as "green." It's relieving to know, however, that I am not alone. I met Custer's bugler, and after a swallow or two of some whiskey, he was sharing stories I can not retell on these pages, but he sympathizes with the Indians who must deal with Custer's leadership, the breaking of treaties, and making of empty promises. It galls me so! But don't fret, dear sister, for now I intend to focus on the obedience that is expected by the military, as well as you. I just hope my values won't soon be tested. I have no regrets. I am certain that I'm following God's plan, that this is where I'm supposed to be. Fort Kearny is the only outpost in these parts not being attacked by Indians. I am proud of this.

7

I lay my head each night with good conscience, and I have come to often think of Uncle George.

And that thought brings me to a philosophical question for you: Is it possible to have a powerful connection with the deceased? I'm feeling a bond with our uncle, a bond beyond the rebellious nature of his letters. Deeper. I think he's trying to talk to me from the other side. After Franz was discharged, his friend Karl was promoted to captain, moving on to Fort Kearny with me, and he talks to his dead father all the time. But he's loony, Liv. I understand that he's still grieving, even after all these years, but Karl's obsessed with his vati. *He thinks he's holding real conversations with the man. I'm not that bad. I just get a strange sense that Uncle George is warning me to stay away from someone or something, and my gut says it's Karl. Before Franz left his service, he was indebted to Karl for saving him, for carrying him to safety after being hit in the leg by Indian fire, but I'm not sold on that soldier. His details of that day don't add up. Franz may be loyal, but I am leery, and I'm glad Franz is on his way back home. If Karl's vati brought us together as military comrades, then I can't help but believe Uncle George is trying to split us up.*

My eyes are blurring, so I must retire. Tell Mother and Father that I am well and think of them often. Tell Franz to write soon, and tell Catherine to be patient with him. Hugs to Junior!

All my love to you, dear sister!
Blessings—
Jonas

CHAPTER 1

"Do I look presentable, Mother? Do I smell all right?"

I remember saying those exact words. *Do I smell all right?* Scents were not a compulsion with me prior to our coming to Chicago. The air and fields back home in Quakertown were taken for granted, a backdrop for my youth, living innocently on the farm. From the moment we stepped foot on city soil, when the winds were traveling toward us along the lakeside, my nostrils have been infiltrated with the stench of slaughter, sewage, and such. Catherine told me it was all in my head, that we didn't even live in the South district nearest the stockyards and packing houses, and the poor Irishmen of that area were the ones who had it the worst, so I shouldn't dare complain. I guess there were some days when the smell seemed normal, when the air was still, when my head ceased to ache, but most days offered the constant reminder that city life might not bring us the hope we thought it would. Jonas' death still haunted us, Franz's post-war depression ensued, and Father's questions about his brother's demise remained unanswered.

Mother wasn't in full agreement with the idea of coming to Chicago, but she followed her husband as he followed his brother's ghost, like the Pied Piper whistling his intoxicating tunes from the heavens above. As for Catherine and me, we were simply glad to make the journey all together. We were cautiously optimistic.

"You look divine," Mother replied, as she slapped at the bottom of my frock to remove a bit of lint. She had tried her best to make my attire as beautiful as could be; after all, our humble clothing usually made us a target for those more fortunate. I remember looking at the ladies' dresses when we arrived that spring day. Father had been warned not to talk to "runners" trying to con us for money. He was fearful of these people and relied on the guidance of Franz, the son of Father's best friend who had been residing with our family for several years. Franz said he knew where to go, that we simply had to head north, over the river, into the northern district where people would know our culture and not take advantage of our ignorance. Of course, I perceived myself as intelligent, not ignorant in the least, and I wanted to take charge and discuss with fellow educated souls the latest books I had read.

When we journeyed up an unknown street in this wondrous city called Chicago, I started out confident, just the way Franz's wife Catherine told me to, but soon I was cognizant of my surroundings, and my head fell as my back slumped. I tried to disappear without a whisper after noticing all of the grand homes and elegant women. This was not Pennsylvania country with rolling fields and distant farms. I felt small, smaller than Junior who skipped down the boulevard and kicked a rock along the wooden planks. Father and Mother were haggard compared to other adults that snickered at us, and Franz dragged our trunk with his face tipped toward the earth, cursing his "ignorance" of the street he had chosen to get to the North side. Catherine looked like a pauper next to the silks and embroidery flowing from the waists of the striking women we passed, but her gait was upright, and she was the only one of us to walk with a fully vertical stride. I wished over and over again that one day I'd have her confidence.

"Now turn around, Livia," Mother told me. "Back straight." And I jumped into alignment when I felt her hand press against my spine. "Yes, simply divine." She smiled at me with that seldom smirk, when the little lines at the corners of her cracked lips were defined, as were the wrinkles on her forehead and neck. I couldn't tell if her expression was one of pride, grief, or disappointment. Any of those emotions were possible; maybe all three were jumbled up inside and being reflected in her cloudy blue eyes.

"Here's your nickel. Now don't tell your father." Usually, the five cent horse-car fare was an extravagance in which we didn't indulge because Father couldn't justify spending a nickel for transportation that equaled the same speed as walking, but Mother and I both knew that I needed to make a good impression, and though riding the box shaped car couldn't save me time, it would surely save my shoes and dress from the muck of the dirty walks and manure ridden streets. Mother and Catherine had been saving their coins for new thread and buttons, but after hearing about my interview, they decided to spare the money.

Mother made the sign of the cross, placed both of her hands on my shoulders, and bowed her head. "Lord, may You be with my child Livia and walk at her side as she ventures out today. May Your will be done, and may we accept the path You intend. I pray we learn to live, sacrifice, and love according to Your plan."

When it came time to bless me, Mother always included a special devotion to the Blessed Virgin. She said that all women could turn to her because she lived in us and understood us better than we could humanly understand ourselves.

"Amen," I replied. Mother remained solemn, but I was joyous.

This was not a typical day in the family shop. I was not going to tidy the stale storefront where the walls absorbed the pungent aroma of smoke samplers. I was not going to crawl on hands and knees beside Catherine, furiously scrubbing at caked and hardened mud adhered to the wooden floor. I was not going to listen to the metal knocking and sliding of Father and Franz as they stripped and pressed the tobacco. I was not going to bend over tables as supervisor to Junior's tedious separating of filler from binder and wrapper leaves. I was not going to tightly roll each cigar into tiny papooses, readied for Mother's molding and packaging into uniform boxes which had been labeled the night before. No. On this day I would be exempt from the monotony of these rote responsibilities, and instead, head out to the heart of the city for a job interview that had nothing to do with the Haas business.

I would stroll down the street and take the horse-car down State Street. I would get off at Randolph and mingle among the rich with my head held high and shoulders back, as Catherine instructed, to blend in and not feel unworthy of my footsteps on their walkways, and if my eyes should meet the gaze of a passerby, I would grin, nod a greeting, and continue on my way toward the celebrated Sherman House where the wealthy businessmen lodged during their stay in this mighty city, and all the while I would think of Jonas and his dreams of escaping the tobacco farm for something more.

I grabbed my copy of *A Tale of Two Cities*, one of the few possessions that had survived our move. I had already read it countless times, but in case I arrived early and had to wait, I wanted Mrs. Sherman to see that I was an honest-to-goodness avid reader, a literate candidate for employment in her highly respected establishment. I opened the book, opened the door, and stepped outside.

"Don't you read while walking, Livia. You'll trip and fall," Junior reprimanded me.

"Thanks for the advice, little man," I giggled, and I leaned over for a quick hug. Being a nine-year-old meant avoiding public displays of affection, but without another hooligan in sight, Junior was safe. "And don't you wander off to that garbage pile down the street, you hear me?"

"I hear you," the boy sulked.

I opened the book again and was on my way. Engrossed in Dickens' tale, I almost strode past my stop. Luckily, the horse-car was just coming down the rails, and with the sound of the horse's clopping atop the wheels rumbling, my mind snapped back to reality. The vehicle came to a halt, startling me even though I had expected its abrupt presence, and I remained motionless.

"Ya comin', Miss?" asked the conductor. My mind was saying yes, but my body was not in line with my thoughts. I tripped on the step and landed hard on my knees. Humiliated at the sight of the driver staring down at me, I demurely leaned to the right to retrieve my skirt from beneath my body, and I lifted the heavy cotton layers to stand. I had no idea how many passengers there were; I wouldn't dare look up from the ground. All I could do was hold my breath and try to collect my composure long enough to find a bench close to the front. Plopping into my seat, I put my head into my hands. *Don't cry, Livia. Don't be hard on yourself.* I felt the warmth of my cheeks against my palms.

"You dropped this."

Don't make things worse. Don't cry.

"Ma'am."

"Don't cry," I accidentally mumbled aloud.

"Excuse me?"

I jolted upright, and with tears teetering on my upper lids, I looked up to find a handsome man with an outstretched hand. His fingers were scratched and stained and calloused, too rough looking for his boyish grin, and his eyes were fresh and clear, a glimmering smoky gray with long eyelashes that continued dancing into the creases.

"I wanted to return this book ya dropped, is all, but doesn't it look like you could use a handkerchief, too?"

"I'm... I'm..." I cleared my throat, and then quietly muttered, "I'm a bit embarrassed." I took the book from his rustic grasp, placed it on my lap, and wiped my face with my fingertips.

"Try this now won't ya?" His brogue was not as thick as some of our Irish customers'.

He was still standing at my side, one hand offering a white

cloth, the other holding on to the ceiling, bracing himself as the horse-car bounced along the tracks.

"Shall I let ya alone ma'am, or shall I lend an ear?"

"Thank you," I replied, and I moved over to let him sit down next to me. He smelled woodsy, for there was a faint scent of pine coming from his arms. I took the handkerchief and looked at it nervously. Of course my nose was congested, and I wanted to blow into it, but I knew I should only use this stranger's possession to wipe my eyes. I patted my cheeks and sat there with the damp rag in my lap.

"You might as well get all the unlucky stuff out of the way early in the day," he said. "Me da tells me that a lot, and it's good advice, eh, 'cause the rest of the day always appears a pleasure then, ya see?"

I looked down at the scuff marks on the edges of my dress. "If the rest of the day actually brings good luck, I suppose."

"Ah, me fair maiden, 'tis good luck indeed."

Can he tell I'm blushing? I tried to glance at him with a smile, but just then a breeze blew strong for a moment, and with the air came the aroma of nearing factories. I sneezed. *Dear God!* I sneezed, unintentionally, directly into the handkerchief. I froze. *I can't possibly return the cloth after soiling it this way!* I started rambling.

"I haven't any money right now to buy you a new one, but if I get this position today, I will purchase a handkerchief with my first pay, or I could simply wash it for you. Yes, I will wash it for you when I get home, and I will return it to you, no, well, yes, I could—" *Stop the gab, Livia.*

15

He chuckled. "Shush now. I won't hear any of that nonsense because it's a gift. A good luck hanky." He patted my arm as to console me. "No wonder you're out of sorts today. For what kind of work are you applying?"

"Servant work at the Sherman House." My response was direct, and I felt proud when saying it and more at ease because this man apparently didn't mind my childish scene. If I was as pitiful as I had thought, he would not still be next to me initiating a conversation.

"Now isn't that ambitious of ya?" he replied. *Ambitious? Do I sense sarcasm?*

"You don't think I could get such employment at a classy place like the Sherman?" I asked indignantly. "You don't even know me. A few female tears and an inexpensive frock, and you think me weak and unworthy, but I'll have you know, mister, I am surely—" *Where was this tone coming from?* A memory of my snapping at Jonas when he'd touched a nerve I didn't realize I had, flashed through my mind.

"No, no, no. Ya got me all wrong," he interrupted. "I work for the Shermans on and off. They give me small contracts for crafting furniture, most recently their entrance parlor chairs. They rarely have openings, is all. You'd think with their wealth, they could hire a few more dedicated workers and lessen the hours of those already employed, but no such luck, ya see?" He continued. "I know many of the servants there. Poor Clementine especially, works too hard for the pittance she gets in return."

"You've met the Shermans?"

"Indeed. I may wish that they'd hire more people, but the Shermans aren't that bad, really. Condescending at times, like many folk of that stature can be, but for the most part, they are cordial."

"That's what I thought, too, when I met Mrs. Sherman at the post office. I was behind her in line, making a cigar delivery," I told him, "and I overheard her telling the clerk that workers these days were lazy and illiterate at home, at the post office, at the library, even. She told him, 'If my book order was placed correctly, my Hawthorne and Dickens would have been ready for pick up at the library, not still at the post office for me to make an extra trip. And now you're telling me they've been misplaced! This is appalling!'"

"So how did ya get to talking to the lady yourself?" he asked.

"When the manager stepped up to the desk with her books, Mrs. Sherman said, 'Such competence is a rare find. Should you ever desire a new position, you can interview at my hotel.' He politely declined, of course, but meanwhile, I mustered up the nerve to ask if she'd be willing to extend the job invitation to a hard working girl who shared her interest in Dickens."

"Bold are ya?"

"I think I summoned up the courage from Jo March, one of my favorite characters."

"And literate, too? *Little Women*, eh?"

"You've read it?"

"I have, and don't I think I like ya, Miss... Miss...?"

"Haas. Livia Haas." And I extended my hand.

"Well, Miss Livia Haas, my name is William Magee, but won't ya do me the honor of calling me Will?"

"I will, Will," I replied with a flirtatious ease I had never experienced before.

Without hearing the bells, I knew it wasn't even seven o'clock in the morning, yet I had already experienced much excitement in meeting Will. The romantic in me wanted to talk about more than my tobacco expertise, but I had just missed the Randolph stop and already had to backtrack by getting off at the next intersection of Washington and State Streets. The horse-car halted, and I had to leave, but I hoped to run into him again. He said he would make sure of it. *How could he be certain? He doesn't even know where I live?* But I had to remain focused on Mrs. Sherman and the job, not a stranger's courtesies.

I walked down Washington Street, and never before had I seen such exquisite architecture, especially that of the newly renovated Crosby Opera House with its Italianate style and enticing arch. I caught myself daydreaming about getting dressed up and meeting Will to attend a performance. *Why am I still thinking about him?* I could not believe that a world such as this existed a short distance from our humble cigar shop. When I turned onto Clark, a hustle and bustle was setting pace around the perimeter of the Courthouse. An impressive iron gate surrounded the grounds, and within the fence were lush trees, manicured lawns, and colorful blossoms in every hue imaginable —lavender bluebells, coral coneflowers, bright yellow black-eyed Susans, pure white hydrangeas. The building itself stood stoically, bright and tall and strong, with a majestic dome housing a bell that started to ring – dong, dong – on and on until the seventh toll sounded. I was still early for my 7:30 a.m. interview at the Sherman House, another grand structure that stared across the street at the Courthouse. I looked up at its six stories, its fine marble façade, and its windows curved in perfect unison row by row, column by column. I tried envisioning myself peering out between the lace curtains, entranced by the entire view of the block before me.

I had to wait in the parlor for Mrs. Sherman. What a magnificent room! I listened to my shoes tapping against the maple floor as I made my way through the arched entryway, and I found a fireplace with a heavy mantel adorned by etched crystal vases filled with fragrant roses. The mirror above this masterpiece with its golden leaves intertwined in a rectangular form, shone brightly against the glare of the chandelier in the center of the ceiling decorated by a mural of angels. I sat down in a comfortable and elegant seat; its high back was cushioned with a thick tapestry of olive and red vines, attached with bronze medallion buttons. Closing my eyes, I saw Will toiling over this chair, a masterpiece unto itself, with its impeccable carving detail. *Could he really have made this piece of furniture? I have got to stop thinking about him! But he said he crafted the parlor chairs.*

"Mrs. Sherman will see you now," said the front desk man.

"Thank you," I replied, and he escorted me to a second floor office where I met with my future employer.

When I walked into the shop, I knew Franz and Junior would be down at the grazing yard with Janie, our neighbor's cow. Father was alone at the counter hovering over "the books," as he called his finance ledger, with his deep set eyes fixated on whatever numbers he was trying to juggle, and the bags under his sockets seemed puffier than usual.

"Where are Mother and Catherine?" I asked, trying to hold back my glee in the presence of Father's apparent gloom. Without ever lifting his gaze, he grunted, "Heinrich's."

Mrs. Heinrich was a woman from the sewing circle, and though they were only new acquaintances, I was sure the visit was a consoling one after hearing that Mr. Heinrich had been laid off from the packing house due to a terrible injury on the job. Sadly, the man lost his thumb and forefinger in a slicing machine. Figuring he would be of no use to them anymore, the company let him go. I was selfishly wishing that Mother or Catherine had been home. I wanted to share my good news with someone, anyone but Father, from the moment Mrs. Sherman said I could start work on Monday "on a temporary basis, for two weeks, with six nine-hour days, one lunch break each day, and weekly pay of $2.50 . . . Missy will meet you at the back door to instruct you of your duties." Oh, it wouldn't be temporary! I stopped listening to the woman after that. All I could think about was earning a few extra dollars for the family, to maybe lessen the burden and prove to Father that my working outside the store could be a good thing, not the crazy idea of a dreamer, which meant anything he didn't deem practical, which was how he viewed Jonas' beliefs. This was the first time I'd be

20

the one to test Father, but our cigar business would not suffer without my help. I would still be around for the daily morning preparations, and I would still make deliveries on my day off, and maybe Franz and Catherine wouldn't have to worry about the pregnancy and having another mouth to feed. This was a great opportunity for all of us.

"I need you to stay here until closing time," he said in a monotone voice as he shut the ledger and placed it under the counter. He took his hat and started toward the door.

"Where are you going?" I asked.

"I have errands. When your mother gets back this evening, tell her not to hold dinner. I'll be gone a while." I was sure he hadn't eaten breakfast, and it was possible he wouldn't eat at all that day, and when I tried to suggest my fixing him a small plate before leaving, Father simply walked out without a response.

Mother was too distraught about Mr. Heinrich to talk when she returned home. I never got to tell her that the job was "temporary," but that didn't matter to me because I was sure I would be kept on anyway. I also never got to tell her about meeting Will, and that was probably a good omission because she would have worried about my meeting strangers… male strangers . . Irish male strangers . . . maybe even Irish male strangers with sinful thoughts. It was better off that our conversation was brief. Catherine, on the other hand, was thrilled for me.

"Livia, this is wonderful news! It's important for you to experience life outside this store. The whole world isn't as humdrum as it is around here, and I have a good feeling that this is just the beginning of great things for you."

"With $2.50 extra each week, you'll not have to worry about that little angel inside you," I explained.

"We'll be fine, Liv. I know we will," and Catherine caught the gleam in my eye. "What are you smiling about?"

"I just thought of something else when you said 'I know we will.'" I couldn't help thinking about him again. I was bursting to share my story of Will.

"You heathen! How dare you not tell me about him even before the job story? Describe him to me, and tell me exactly what he said, in his brogue and all," she said while clapping her hands.

She told me not to get my hopes too high about seeing him again, but the story of meeting a gentleman and experiencing the seeds of a relationship brought back memories of when she first met Franz and how carefree they were at one time. A quietness came over her. "The war changed him some, hardened his heart a bit." She sighed. "Slowly but surely, though, Liv, I feel him coming back to me. We still have a spark that I hope will remain forever lit, so I pray we'll continue to have our hearts and ears open to listen."

Catherine always had a way with words. Me? I was just plain giddy.

CHAPTER 2

On Sunday morning, we attended mass at St. Michael and then headed over to Washington Square for the weekly picnic. A customary event for German families in our neighborhood, these festivities provided time for escape from the previous week's stresses. Even the stinky air seemed unnoticeable because there were too many other distractions to rid one's mind of the odor, like music and dancing, food and drink and games, and as always, some kind of political talks being carried from group to group. Though some men refused to speak of work on Sundays, others took advantage of the gathering to debate and question the issues of the day. Father rarely started out taking part in these lively discussions, but once he had a mug or two, his hostility got the best of him, and suddenly the quiet soul became a man of strong opinions, and he ranted on and on. I gave up the attempt to participate in these dialogues. The men never appreciated my input, and many felt obligated to soften their vocabulary in my presence, thereby losing their verbal passion of ardent debate. I opted to eavesdrop while pretending to read on a nearby bench or behind one of the larger elms. Frequently, I'd jot down topics of concern during the more heated discussions and think of Jonas, but sometimes, I would let it alone and simply join the women's talk to avoid female scrutiny because they, too, didn't look kindly on my mingling in male antics. However, no matter people's opinion, picnics inspired my writing, especially when I was reminded of my brother, and I'd scribble thoughts into my journal.

our lives are in a state of war from birth
—a hero's cry is heard with trembling tongue—
until our buried bones adorn the earth
—another rebel yell silenced too young—

When we arrived at the park, Mother was greeted by neighborhood seamstresses who were arranging meals to be sent to the Heinrich house. Franz excused himself almost immediately and left to meet up with friends from Turner Hall. Father strolled only a few feet before his name was called from the beer garden. Catherine and I took Junior to the pony rides and found a clearing next to a shade tree. We set down the blanket and opened our basket— Mother's warm pretzels, fresh strawberries and juicy melon wedges, *Leaves of Grass* by Walt Whitman. I took the book and looked at Catherine quizzically.

"I thought we'd read together, like old times," replied my friend. "That is, after you tell me more about your adventure yesterday." She straightened the edges of the hand sewn patchwork, scraps of varying shapes and sizes left behind from sewing projects that Catherine reconfigured to design her own picnic throw. "With the exception of our brief chat last evening, you haven't told me anything about the Sherman House. Was the hotel as beautiful as everyone says? How long did it take to get there by horse-car?" I must have blushed without response. "Livia Haas, you can't keep your mind off of him, can you?" she jested.

I sat down beside her. "I *can*, but I don't know of anything better to think about."

Catherine conceded. "Ha! Go ahead and tell me more. His name is Will, right?"

"Yes, his name is Will. And for some reason, I feel as if I already know him. That's strange, right? But Catherine, he was easy to talk to. We could have chatted for hours. Could it have been fate that we met?"

"Fate, eh?" The voice came from behind the tree, and when Will popped his head around the corner, my face turned redder than it did in the horse-car incident, and my heart was about to burst right out of my chest. "Will!" I exclaimed.

Catherine stood for introductions. "Hello, Mr. Magee," she said, foisting her hand out straight. "I am Livia's friend, Catherine."

"The maiden is a bit frazzled, I'd say now, isn't she Miss Catherine?"

"Yes, I'd say so. It's a pleasure to meet you, Will."

"Likewise."

I fixated on Will's face. His cleft chin reminded me of a heart from this angle.

"Livia, are you feeling all right?" she asked.

"What are you doing here?" My fingers trembled while my palms sweated, and Whitman tumbled to the ground. Will knelt down to retrieve the book.

"Now don't ya have to stop this habit of dropping fine literature? How can I keep saving these stories from ruin?" I was mesmerized by his gray eyes. "I told you we would meet again, eh?" he whispered.

"How did you know I'd be here?"

"Didn't I mention I was a carpenter by day and a spy by night?" He laughed and stood to turn to Catherine. "I'm joking of course, but didn't I work like the devil to see her again."

"You must have." She smiled and then excused herself to go check on her son.

"May I stay?" he asked.

"Of course I want you to stay, but I'd rather my parents not see us, so would you mind if we took a walk away from the picnic?" Will nodded and helped me stand.

I led us toward Clark Street, and once out of sight of the picnickers, I asked, "Really Will, how did you know where to find me?"

"I'd be lying if I said I wasn't lookin' for ya. I figured you lived in the North district, since ya got on the horse-car up north, and your name is Haas which led me to believe that you had German blood, and since many Northsiders attend these Sunday picnics, you were bound to be here, weren't ya?"

"Besides, this isn't my first picnic. I've got carpenter friends of all nationalities, and I've been invited to a German picnic or two in the past. Not today, of course, but don't I fulfill my promises, eh?"

"You do, and for that I am thrilled more than you know." We walked a bit with an awkward silence. "So what are the names of your carpenter friends?"

"Do you know John Olson?" Will asked. I said that I did. "We belong to the same Carpenters' Union. He and a number of representatives are in attendance here, ya know, even some union leaders. Though I'm a lowly Irishman," he teased, "I'm also indebted to the men who strive to bring fairness to the workers' plight, eh?"

"Sounds to me like you're an agitator, Mr. Magee," I replied as we continued to stroll south on Clark.

"Agitator ya say? Not really. I'm proud to have participated in a few strikes with me da, but it's disheartening when good intentions are stomped on time and time again, and that's the case in the fight for the eight-hour day."

"If you are not rebellious, how exactly would you describe your relationship with the leadership here at the picnic? They are definitely rabble-rousers in our community."

"Ya seem to know a thing or two about agitators, Miss Haas. Has your father ever been involved with them?"

"Not with these men in Chicago. He doesn't get involved much except when he's had a drink," I laughed.

"Watch your step, eh?" Will touched my elbow to warn me of the missing plank on the walkway. I stepped over the opening.

"Thanks."

Returning his hand to his trouser pocket, he smiled and squinted into the sun. "So, the drink can turn your da into a radical."

"He'll talk a good talk at the picnics, and that's the extent of it, but his brother George died an agitator, and I think my uncle takes over Father's brain when he drinks. If Uncle George was alive, you'd see him up on the soapbox at these gatherings, trying to corral fresh blood to join his cause."

"Uncle George, eh?"

"He and Father and their closest friend left Bavaria and settled in Pennsylvania, but Quakertown was much too tame for Uncle George. As soon as he heard about this city with all the opportunity and action, he didn't hesitate to take the next train west." We stopped to let a horse-car pass before crossing the street. "Unfortunately, Chicago didn't treat him very well. As Uncle George put it in one of his letters, he "underestimated the control of the establishment," and when he realized he was living in the shadows of the Protestant upper class, he wrote further about the workers' miseries."

"When we met, you spoke of your family cigar shop. Was he, too, in the business?"

"Oh, yes. As far as I know, tobacco is the sole trade of all my relatives. It's what we know and do well, and Uncle George was in the Cigar Makers' Union, I'll have you know."

"Ah, I'd have liked him. Me own family's been carvin' since the beginnin' o' time, they say. Back in Ireland, the Magee men were known to marry the lumberjack ladies for professional partnerships, eh?"

"Practical, but not very romantic."

Will clasped his hands behind his back and leaned forward in his stride. The bending posture made me feel as if he was listening intently and speaking directly to me. "I agree. Not romantic at all." I pointed to the right to make a turn at the corner. "How long ago did your uncle die?"

"I was quite young. I rarely saw him in person before he left, but I've read all of his correspondence. Father doesn't like talking about his brother, but I believe that Father agreed to come to Chicago for closure. He never did find out where Uncle George was buried."

"I'm intrigued by this man. How did Uncle George come to pass?"

"From what we could make of the situation, he was involved in a riot back in '55."

"The Lager Beer Riots, eh?" Will asked.

"Yes, and though only two people died, Uncle George was seriously injured. He wrote that the police started raising the bridge while the protesters were crossing, and my poor uncle's leg got crushed under a fallen horse. He couldn't walk or work, and he ended up lingering on in pain while an infection spread."

"I'm sorry, Liv."

"Father was devastated when his last letter to Chicago was returned with a simple word written across Uncle George's address—DEAD. We don't even know who sent the note back to us. Jonas believed that whoever wrote on the envelope was someone who delighted in our uncle's passing."

"Jonas?"

"My brother. He died of pneumonia in '67. He was only 21, stationed along the westward paths in Nebraska. Jonas had lots of opinions, so he and Uncle George had lots in common."

"Well, wasn't I right then, when I said ya knew a thing or two about agitators?"

Later that night, when extinguishing the last candle in the house, I sat at the kitchen table and stared at the swirling strand of white smoke as it lifted away from the wick's red bead of fire.

In the dark, I imagined our Pennsylvania home and Jonas, the agitator, in the chair across from me, explaining his need to enlist, even if he had not been summoned, even if the war was close to an end . . .

"You don't understand, Liv. There's a fire inside me, a burning to stand for what's right, not out of obligation and obedience like Franz, but because it's simply the right thing to do. Our cause is ethical and righteous, and each day I'm a civilian instead of a soldier, my spirit is being stifled."

"Is there no fire," I asked, "not even a spark, to do what's right by your family in staying home? That choice is just as honorable, Jonas."

"Honor? I'm not searching for honor. I want to know at the end of each day that I've done my part in ensuring some kind of justice. Do you realize how slaves are treated? Have you any idea the brainwashing and brutal force that must be happening in order to get these men to fight for the Confederacy against their own freedom? Do you know the lies being told to and about the Indians, as well? Liv, the Indians are being bribed into war, being told that they'll be rewarded with land, land that was taken from them in the first place. No such reward will be granted, but there's a whole culture of ignorance out there that has dehumanized these Indians and slaves."

I rolled my eyes at the word dehumanized. "You know what I'm thinking when you talk that way, don't you, Jonas?"

"That I'm like Uncle George?" He smiled a recognizable, mischievous grin, the one when he rose his eyebrows into the middle of his forehead. "Did it ever occur to you, Livia, that our

30

father, too, was like Uncle George when he participated in that liberal fest in Bavaria? Or when he stood up against the Know-Nothings in Philadelphia? Both Uncle George and Father rubbed elbows with the 48ers, but our father stopped all that when we were born. He didn't want to take risks when kids were at stake, and I respect his parental decisions, but don't let him convince you that Uncle George was the only rebellious Haas. It's hereditary, dear sister, and the bug will get you, too, mark my word. The only question is whether or not you'll be willing to take arms."

"And you are willing?" I asked.

"At first I worried about it. But even after reading Franz's correspondence from the trenches, something has changed in me, and I want nothing more than to join. I think I've been called."

"You mean a higher calling?"

"Yes," he replied with certainty. "It's hard to explain." He leaned back in his chair, momentarily contemplative before returning his body close to the table. "Don't you ever feel called to do something bigger than this? To be more than a farmhand or house servant?"

"I'm already more than that, Jonas. I am a daughter with devotion to my family, and I am content with this, as should you be," was my retort.

"Contentment is not an option." He looked straight at me, staring into my soul. "What do you desire, Livia? Truly desire. I mean, what would complete you?"

Complete you. *I had never thought of myself as incomplete.*

"Your dreams, Liv," my brother expounded. "Don't tell me

you don't have dreams."

"Of course, I have dreams," I replied. "But I can be whole without achieving pointless whimsies. I'm a rational person, Jonas, so I understand that nothing becomes of dreams. Nothing."

"I disagree. All things are possible."

"For whom?" I asked. Suddenly, the words flowed from my mouth, as if the thought had been with me for years. "For you, maybe, all things are possible because dreaming of being a soldier when our country is at war is called fate. That's no dream, Jonas. Try being the female child of a tobacco farmer with no connections or financial means to get a real education. Well, now, how about that for a dream?"

My words hung in the air before I heard a muffled chuckle.

"What's so funny?" I demanded.

"Oh, it's not funny, Livia. Your message is not funny at all," he replied still grinning. "It's just that I knew I'd get it out of you."

"Great. You win."

"I did not intend for this discussion to be a game. I am no more victorious as you are defeated, dear sister."

"All I'm saying, Jonas, is that wants and dreams are two different things. If I want to keep learning, I will do so through personal reading and writing, every chance I get. Isn't that good enough? If I was adamant about achieving a dream, I'd become bitter about education, and maybe I'd lose interest all together. Why should I dwell on dreams, when I could be just as content with realistic wants?"

32

"You think you'll find happiness in running the farm forever?" he asked.

"If that's God's plan, then I will remain content."

"But will you be happy?"

"Good night, Jonas."

I remember closing my eyes when my head hit the pillow that night, but I never slept.

CHAPTER 3

On my first day of employment, I arrived at the back
entrance of the Sherman House and was met by a petite, slight
woman with a dark caramel complexion. She spoke before I
could introduce myself.

"Now don't you be standin' 'round with yer jaw all dropped.
We ain't got no time for that. Come on in an' let's git goin'."
Chastised, I didn't know how to respond in any other way but to
follow her, silently, as she led me down a short corridor to a
dimly lit changing room. "Yer uniform's in that closet over
there, so git a move on, an' I'll meet you next door in the
kitchen." She was tiny, so tiny that if I saw her from behind I
would think she was a child of maybe eleven or twelve, but from
the front side, her face and voice told me otherwise. She was
small in stature but tough.

My uniform was a plain black dress with oversized sleeves
and a puffy bustle. The shoulders hung low, and the waist was
too wide while the bottom dropped to the floor. "Whoo-eee,"
she laughed when I walked into the kitchen. "Ya look like an
orphan young'un in that thang." I started to mumble an
explanation of the problems I was having, when she threw an
apron at me.

"Stop all that whining, girl, an' jus put this apron on. No
one'll notice anyways 'cause I'm the only one gonna be lookin'
at ya."

"But I don't feel comfortable at all," I complained.

"Comfortable? Well, if yer thinkin' this job is gonna be one of comfort, I'm thinkin' you applied for the wrong position."

"I didn't mean that. I just meant that I could probably do a better job if I wasn't pulling and tugging at my clothes all day."

"So don't pull and tug," she said flatly. "Enough of this chattin'. We gots work to do." With that she was at the kitchen counter passing piles of vegetables at me to wash, peel, trim, and cut. Each carrot needed to be a certain length, each potato sliced to a specific width, each green bean blanched for a set time, and so on, with no room for mistakes and waste, and this continued for nearly two hours with Missy—as I soon learned her name—coming and going with no discussion unless she was giving orders or I was asking questions. For some strange reason, I actually liked her. I liked her work ethic, I liked her grit, I liked her attention to detail. Missy was obviously not one of the inept employees Mrs. Sherman grumbled about in the post office. As a matter of fact, for a slight colored woman to have a supervisory position, she must have been the worker who set the bar high for employee expectations, and for this I respected her.

I tried my best to keep up while not pulling and tugging at my uniform. She assigned kitchen duties all morning, and at noon she said I could take a fifteen minute lunch break, that I could take it out back in the small courtyard where the guests would not see me. "What about you, Missy? Will you join me?" I asked. Her face gave a bewildered expression with narrowed eyes and scrunched nose.

"You worry 'bout yer own self, an' I'll worry 'bout mines," she replied, and she went back to shucking a basket of corn.

I took off my apron, placed it on a hook near the pantry,

retrieved my lunch pail, and headed toward the door. Then I heard her voice, more faint than any other words she had spoken all morning. "But thanks for askin'," she said under her breath. I smiled and exited the room.

Outside, I used a large decorative rock as my seat and took out my hard-boiled egg, tomato, and cucumber slices. *Dear Lord, I pray that I am competent. Thank you for the food before me, and thank you for this opportunity. Mother Mary, give me grace and patience when dealing with Missy.*

"Peach?"

"Ach!" I yelled out, startled by the intrusive sound.

"Shhhh," said Will with his forefinger pressing up on his lips.

"You've got to stop doing that, Will," I whispered. "What are you doing here?"

"I told ya I worked for the Shermans before, so I thought I'd stop by to check on the inventory, see if I'm needed for another assignment." When I did not respond, he added, "And to see how your day was going."

I looked to my left and to my right, grateful to have no one else around. "Well, it was going fine," I started. "But I'll be terminated before the day's out if I'm found here with you. You must leave."

"Clementine said I could be here, and Mrs. Sherman likes me, ya see. She wouldn't think anything of the fact that I was coming by because I check in with her every now and then for projects."

"First of all, I do not know Clementine. I only know a

woman by the name of Missy who has been distant and demanding for the past four and a half hours. It was just now that she softened, and I don't want to mess this up, Will."

"Is there a second of all?" he asked grinning.

"Second of all, Mrs. Sherman may like you, but she hardly knows me at all, so I wish you would not spoil my relationship with her before I even *form* a relationship with her."

"Very well, then, Livia. I hope ya have a good day," he said and tipped his hat before continuing, "and when you meet Clementine, please give her my regards, eh." As he turned to go, I touched his elbow.

"Will, please, I don't mean to be short with you, but I just don't want to take any chances on my first day. You understand, don't you? I'm truly flattered that you're here. I am. I would give anything to spend this time with you, but I just don't think this is a good idea."

"Okay," he replied before taking and kissing my hand. "When can I see ya again?"

"I don't know, but I'm confident you'll figure that out." The flirtatious smile flashed across my face without thinking about it.

Will did not return at lunchtime that first week. I found myself looking around the courtyard, anticipating another peach offering, waiting to see him again. *Did I end things before they even had a chance to begin? Was I being too cautious? Was I rude?* How odd it was to feel strongly about a stranger. Come Saturday, Missy gave me a welcomed distraction from Will-withdrawal when she handed me a package.

"Just a little somethin' for ya. Break's over," she said and then retreated to the kitchen.

I opened the package and found a new black dress into which I immediately ran in the house and changed. It fit me beautifully. When Missy saw me, she gave an approving nod and started right in on peeling the carrots.

"Did you do this, Missy?" I asked.

"Who else woulda done it?" she said.

"Well, I am grateful. This must have been a lot of work, and to spend that kind of time sewing a new uniform for someone who might not even stay on here at the Sherman— I'm almost speechless at your generosity."

"Now that the uniform fits, you can be seen by the guests. We'll git you outta the kitchen once in a whiles, an' don't be worryin' 'bout unemployment; you'll be stayin," Missy replied, never lifting her head from the vegetables.

"Really? How do you know? Did Mrs. Sherman say that?" I could hardly calm my voice.

"Now don't git all crazy on me, girl. I told Mrs. Sherman that I like ya and that yer better than lotsa others that she's hired and fired. I told her we should take a chance on ya an' offer you a permanent job."

"Oh, Missy, thank you, thank you, thank you!" and when I hugged her, her head got smushed against my neck.

"It ain't jus' me you need to be thankin'. Ya better be givin' that kinda hug to my friend Willie, too. He's the one who keeps a tellin' me how good ya is, an' how smart ya is."

"Willie? You mean Will? Was he here? Do you know

him?"

"I known Willie for a long time, girl. Lots of us workers do, and if I didn't like ya then I woulda told him to give up on ya." She shook her head, "Now there's a good man that Willie, mm-hmm, a good man. For a white boy, he's a mighty good man."

"I couldn't agree with you more, Missy. I just wish I could see him again. Did he tell you when he would be back?"

"A little birdie tells me he's a workin' on a new project for Mrs. Sherman. I'm a thinkin' he'll be 'round next week."

"Really?"

"Stop askin' silly questions. I ain't gossipin' wit ya, so jus' git back to work 'fore I change my mind an' tell the Shermans yer not worth the job."

I didn't care how long I had to stay that day. I was humming and singing and practically driving Missy insane with my enthusiastic work. It was about 6:15 when I received my first pay. I stared at my name on the envelope, felt the smooth paper and carefully opened the triangular flap. $2.50.

"Thanks again, Missy, and have a wonderful day off tomorrow," I said to my friend.

"No more thankin' an' I'll be seein' ya Monday."

I gave her another hug just before walking toward the door.

"And bys the way, Livia, my real name's Clementine."

"You are *Clementine*?" I asked. "Why didn't you tell me?"

"Only true friends are allowed to call me bys my real name, an' it took ya this time 'fores I knew I could call you a true friend."

"Will spoke of you. YOU! I can't believe you are

Clementine. Is Missy a nickname?"

"A nickname, mm-hmm," she said grinning. "It's a name for anyone who's not my true friend. Them people gotta address me with a little more respect."

"But *Missy* doesn't sound respectful."

"Jus' think 'bout it on yer day off, girl, an' I'll be seein' ya on Monday."

"Bye Miss . . . I mean Clementine," and I was waving my hand when it hit me. *Miss* C.

I hadn't even approached the back door when the aroma drifting from the windows filled my nose and heart with a sense of family and home. The "old country" foods, blaukraut and kartoffelknodel, could be smelled from across the yard—the butter-fried red cabbage cooked to crispy perfection, the potato dumplings boiled to the right consistency. Mother was a fine Bavarian cook, and about once a month, she still spoiled us with traditional cuisine, just the way I remembered her doing in Pennsylvania. My mouth watered as I entered the kitchen, and my insides jumped with renewed hunger. What a great evening this would be, a fine meal and payday!

Mother and Father were sitting down to dinner when I waltzed in, fanning myself with the pay envelope. "Your first check, I presume," said Mother as she rose to get another place setting.

"Yes, the full $2.50. No scams, no fines, no hidden withdrawals, just the amount I was promised during my interview," I retorted so that Father couldn't hate the Shermans the way he loathed the owners of the yards where many of his acquaintances were employed.

"You'll have forty-five cents to do as you please. Then give your mother the five cents you owe her, and I'll put the rest towards the bills." I glanced at my mother, horrified that Father knew about the horse-car from my first day.

"From here on, if you want to live a luxurious lifestyle like the Shermans, you'll pay for it out of your own pocket, not your mother's." Father glared at me, "And don't try hiding things from me. Do you understand?"

"It won't happen again," I said, losing my appetite, my happy bubble bursting.

Mother broke the thick and lingering silence. "Sit down, Livia. It's time to pray."

"Oh, I don't know what to do about this job, Catherine," I confessed that evening after we had tidied up the shop and took a seat on the front stoop.

"What do you mean? You just started. You're not thinking about quitting, are you?"

"No, I'm not thinking of quitting, but I feel guilty about my parents, as if it's wrong to be happy while they're miserable."

"That's rubbish, Livia. Do you hear yourself? There's no sin in finding happiness."

"My life is now torn between two opposite worlds— excessive and minimal. It's hard to describe, but I get a kind of happy energy from the Shermans' lavish surroundings, and that turns sad and tiresome when I walk into this sparse space. On top of that, I know it's only been a week, but upon my return home each night, Father exudes depression, and Mother exudes exhaustion. Even when filled with pride and excitement tonight, Father managed to strip my smile within an instant, and Mother didn't even speak up on my behalf."

Catherine took my hand in hers and turned toward me. "I won't talk badly about your parents, Liv. They have my eternal respect and gratitude for taking us in and treating us as family." She rubbed the backside of my fingers and looked down at them. "Before my father-in-law Hans died, he described the man who had been his best friend, the man who promised to take care of Franz and me, and the first thing he told us was to appreciate Otto's realistic nature, because it was the saving grace that kept him on his toes. Your uncle George's, also. Hans and George were the idealists of the trio, the ones who were tempted to cross lines, but it was your father who always reined them in." Catherine squeezed my knuckles together and smiled. "That's what he's doing with you, too. Otto is a serious man. He does not want you to feel guilt, but he *does* want you to be pragmatic with your paycheck. That's all."

I let her words sink in.

"Any words of wisdom about Mother?" I asked.

"I know your mother is proud."

"And how would you know that?"

"When we were knitting the other night, she said she was more than pleased that you found a job that has nothing to do with sewing or factory work."

"She never told me that."

42

"That's because you were gone long hours each day this past week. You didn't get to spend as much time with her. That's the only bad part of this whole deal, Livia, and guess what? That's reality. That's life. Everyone ends up spending more time with coworkers than their own families. Luckily, you like your coworkers."

Coworkers. My eyes drifted away from Catherine's steady gaze and down to our linked fingers. I released the hold and smiled.

"Thank you," I said, looking away.

"No more guilt then, right?"

Letting out a sigh, I leaned forward, straightening my skirt, drying the sweat from my hands. "I guess I wasn't being honest with myself about the source of my guilt."

"What do you mean?"

"You said I was lucky to like my coworkers."

"Yes?"

I cleared my throat. "Will is working for the Shermans."

"What?" Catherine exclaimed. "Have you seen him again?"

"He'll start next week. It's just a brief assignment to design a few pieces of hotel furniture. Nonetheless, he feels like a secret, and that must be why I feel guilty."

"This is exciting news, Liv! Who cares if he's a secret! You haven't done anything wrong."

"I'm uneasy. Anxious."

"Of course, anxious! That's what makes this stage of a relationship so special."

"Relationship?"

"Listen, Livia. You don't have to share your every move with the family. My advice is to wait and see how this goes, and if you and Will move toward a relationship beyond walks and talks, then you should introduce him to Otto and Johanna. Until then, don't worry and simply enjoy the *now* of it. Will is God's blessing to you, not a curse."

I wanted to continue the discussion, but just then Catherine grabbed my hand and placed it on her rounding stomach.

"The baby's kicking," she beamed. "Can you feel that?"

I felt a miraculous quiver beneath my fingertips. Another child was going to enter this world and call my dear friend, Mama.

CHAPTER 4

Bent over the kitchen sink with a scrub brush, I didn't notice his entrance, but I felt a slight touch on my shoulder at the same time as I felt his breath on my ear.

"Missy says you need to do some garden gathering," he whispered.

Will was standing at my side with two baskets hanging from his forearm and a proud smirk upon his face.

"I've already been assigned an assistant?" I teased.

It only took a moment to tidy my spot and follow him to the garden.

"After you." Will stopped just before the arbor entrance, an arched opening with purple curtains of climbing wisteria and clematis.

"Whenever I step through this passageway," I said, "I feel as if it's a gateway to another place and time."

"How so?"

I led us to the left, the gravel path crunching beneath the soles of our feet with a trail of allium in full bloom along the cedar fence.

"I'm not a city girl at heart. I grew up among green fields and hills, surrounded by our own fruit trees, vegetable gardens, farm animals. I relish those days. Though the labor was just as constant as here, no sunrise or sunset could compare to those I remember from Quakertown. The skies created a painter's dream of colors, and the shadows cast by Haycock Mountain creeped slowly across the fields, like a blanket removed in the morning or pulled up for a snug tucking in at night."

He handed me one of the baskets. "You're poetic."

"I dabble with words."

We strolled past the trellises of tomatoes and peppers, each an end cap to rows of root vegetables and leaf lettuces.

"We can start at the western side for herbs and berries, and then we'll work our way back."

"When do you find time to write?" he asked.

"At night, mostly. Just brief vignettes and poems about the places and people I never want to forget. Sometimes it's simply details that I might refer back to at a later time. Sometimes it's a prayer or journal entry about my day. Writing brings me peace, so I attempt to jot down whatever's on my mind."

The wall of herbs appeared: rosemary, parsley, thyme, basil, mint. I took out pieces of string from my apron pocket and held them out.

"A bundle of each should do," I smiled.

He took the strings and my fingers, together, bringing them to his face.

"I think you're beautiful," he said and kissed the back of my hand, all the while looking up at me.

"I'll start on the berries," was my nervous response, and I quickly turned toward the strawberry bushes down the aisle.

Franz and Karl were standing on either side of the back stairs, each with a hand resting on the wooden rails, the other hand holding a cigar. Their appearances were opposite in subtle ways, like the parts in their hair. While Franz sported a side part, the humidity puffing up the right half of his head with its thick brown waves, Karl's blond hair was already thinning and receding. Greasy wisps clung across his high forehead with unkept sideburns and mustache framing a once-too-often broken nose and deep set, dark brown eyes. Roughly the same height and weight, Franz's shoulders hunched, while Karl's were broad and straight, making him seem more muscular and controlled.

"Good day at the Sherman, Livia?" asked Karl with a suspicious snarl.

"The same as always, Karl. I'm tired." I didn't look at him.

"Have yourself a short rest, Liv. I think your mother and Catherine have dinner covered," replied Franz, and he stepped aside to give me room to walk the staircase.

"Thanks," I said, avoiding his friend's stare, though I could feel those beady eyes on me.

I let the back door slam behind me.

"Must he stay for dinner?" I questioned Catherine, shivering. "I can't stand being in his company."

I remembered when we first arrived in Chicago. It was Karl who was hospitable and welcoming, and he helped us get settled by finding a business establishment with an attached home. The storefront on the main level was small but had enough room to build a glass counter to house the cigar samples as well as several boxed varieties. The back area was a larger, open space giving us plenty of floor to set up stations for fresh tobacco bins, leaf stripping and pressing, scrap catchers, rolling tables, and shelving for moulds, wrappers, and incoming cigar boxes. Karl couldn't get enough praise for his part in finding the place. "Not

every business comes with a big front window like this one,
Otto. No sir. That's like free advertising, ain't it?" He reminded
my father of this each time he came to pick up Franz to go to
Turner Hall. We thanked him again, of course, and to our thanks
he replied, "No, no, no. No thanks necessary. Just a warm meal
once in a while would be a great token of appreciation that I
would gladly accept, but there's no need for this continued
'thanks.'" For months Karl stopped over at least three times a
week to partake in any meal my mother and I scraped together.
He came early, staring at me with a twitch in his eye while I
cooked, and that made me uncomfortable. He looked me up and
down, and I told my parents I didn't ever want to be alone with
him. Father thought I was over-exaggerating, but Mother agreed
to be with me whenever Karl visited. In either case, Franz still
said he owed Karl his life, and we couldn't possibly create
trouble. I was grateful that the Lord seemed to answer my
prayers, when Karl's appearance became less frequent in recent
weeks, but there he was again, and I was furious.

"At least it's been a while since his last visit," Catherine
replied as she reached for the cupboard.

I stepped in front of my friend and gave her belly a kiss.
"Don't exert yourself. I can do that." I took out seven plates.

"Make it six, Liv. Your father said we shouldn't hold our
meal."

"Again? I swear he doesn't eat anything anymore. He
worries me."

Just then Mother called out to Franz to fetch Junior and wash
up for dinner.

I sighed. "I dread this right now, but I look forward to telling you later about who I saw today."

"You saw Will?"

"He thinks I'm beautiful."

CHAPTER 5

The carts and wagons lined up along Halsted. Blocks away, Junior and I trudged through the dense fog of dust and dirt stirred up by the shuffle of horseshoe and human foot still trekking to the marketplace. Once amidst the chaotic scene, every sensory detail was on overload, especially scents blowing from side to side between sweet peppers of orange, yellow, and green with soured pork gone bad in the autumnal sun. Like a harmonica in the market's band, a train whistle in the distance commenced the day's business song. A harmony of washboard-playing wagon wheels, the rhythmic drumming of hoof taps, the triangle pings of mason jars packed with pickled treasures—the music of market day was a gratifying tune, and Junior's favorite pitch came from the vocal peanut vendor and his tempting lyrics, "Cinnamon coated, perfectly toasted!" or "Get 'em while they're hot!" Junior was beckoned without fail, lured further by the strumming sound of scoops pouring roasted nuts into bags of tasty goodness.

Having noticed a youngster, not much taller than Junior, who visited the same stands as us without a single purchase, I asked, "Do you know that boy in the forage cap?"

Junior looked back at the lettuce cart and the huddled customers grabbing at bunches of romaine, arugula and red leaf. He spied the boy in question. "Sure. Everyone knows Frederick."

"Is he a nice lad?"

"Don't know if he's nice, but he sure is fast. He's the fastest kid in our school. Everyone wants to be on his team for relay races, and people say he goes to Turner Hall and learns gymnastics, too, with the rings and bars and vaulting horse. Isn't that somethin'?"

He tilted his head back and brought the peanut bag high in the air. The last nut made a direct fall into his wide opened mouth, and Junior crumbled the paper bag into a ball while he sucked the salt from the final shell.

"Why are you asking about Frederick?"

"Nothing, really. I just noticed him at the same stands and never saw him before."

I drifted toward the spice wagon with its mixed aromas climbing through my nose, planting their seeds in my mind and transporting thoughts to Mother's fine meals when all the right ingredients were at hand: marjoram, white pepper, juniper berries.

"Do you think my dad might take me to Turner some day?"

Half of me was paying attention to Junior while the other half concentrated on a handful of caraway seeds, "If you ask, he might."

"Jonas likes gymnastics, too."

I stopped in my tracks, letting the seeds drift through my fingers. Surely, Junior meant that as a question. He couldn't possibly remember Jonas. "Yes, Jonas liked gymnastics."

"I know. Sometimes I have memories of him teaching me to somersault through the tobacco rows. And sometimes he talks to me in my dreams." Junior stepped atop a crate and started to play with his paper ball, up and catch, and up and catch.

Is it possible to have a powerful connection with the deceased?

"What does he say?" I asked, as if this was a natural thing, Jonas' ghost talking to Junior in his dreams.

"I remember the messages he sends, like not sulking when I go to church or remembering to help my mother. I forget the exact words by the time I wake up, but I know I refer to him as *uncle*, even though he wasn't my dad's brother, only his best friend."

"Well, that makes sense. I used to call your grandfather, Onkel der Hans because he and my father and my blood uncle were like the Bavarian *Three Muskateers*. They didn't have to have the same mother to be brothers."

"I remember that book! What an adventure!"

"Yes, that's a wonderful story. We should reread it sometime."

"Would Karl be the third muskateer for Jonas and my dad?"

I snatched the paper ball in mid-air. "No, Junior. Not at all."

CHAPTER 6

Shades of gold and copper dotted the landscape, where lush grasses turned to fields of thirsty straw, where emerald leaves drained to scorched amber, and the temperatures dipped to a bearable degree. I appreciated this kind of morning more than the sweltering summer dawns, especially since we hadn't gotten much rain to relieve the hot August nights that led to hot September nights, and it was fitting that such a beautiful day would begin with Clementine handing me a note.

I started opening the envelope when she grabbed my wrist and explained. "Put that aways fer right now. You can read it on yer break." I placed the note in my pocket and began slicing and dicing.

"Who is it from, Miss *C*?" I asked.

Clementine smiled as she worked. "Don't know what ya talkin' 'bout, Liv. I ain't got nothin'. Don't even know hows to read," and then she switched the subject to my new schedule for the day. I'd work in the kitchen until lunch, and then I'd be sent to the parlors and libraries—plural.

"There's a second library?"

"This would be Mr. Sherman's personal room. Not much was done with it since the man passed away last November, but Mrs. Sherman says it's time to give it a good cleaning."

"Where is it, Clem?"

Clementine drew a layout of the specific parlors that needed my attention and explained the best route to complete my tasks, concluding with the personal library. This was a different floor from what I was accustomed, and there was a better chance than normal that I would be seen by hotel patrons. She rambled on for nearly fifteen minutes about the protocol of servants and the appropriate manners involved when dealing with residents of the house.

By the time I got to the new library, it was nearly 5:00. My plan was to dust and polish the furniture, beat the rugs, and tend to the books last, a little reward for myself at the day's end; however, once I fixated on the shelved titles while dusting, the rugs went to the wayside.

Small in size compared to the main library, Mr. Sherman's room was a compact oyster filled with hidden pearls peeking out from every inch of space, secret treasures calling me to visit. Oh, even the musty smell of aged pages left unturned didn't bother me! Books graced the end tables, books wall-papered the floor-to-ceiling shelves, books rested low in racks. They were everywhere, but my first focused glance was on a rare edition of *Uncle Tom's Cabin* by Harriet Beecher Stowe, still splayed to Mr. Sherman's last read and sitting center on his captain's desk in the corner of the room. Jonas loved that story; therefore, I gravitated to its pages to read just a section. Being ever so careful, I lifted the book and took in a deep breath. I let my fingers touch the words of the first page. How delicate the paper! It was an honor to have this tender moment, a kind of intimacy with a master storyteller, and there beneath my fingertips was her signature. *How did I get so lucky?*

"Found something you like, dear?"

I nearly dropped the book, but I had enough control to set it back on the desk without incident. "Pardon?"

"The book. You are in my father's study, and you are holding one of his books. Don't think it wouldn't be noticed if it went missing."

What did Clem say about talking? "Don't be lookin' in people's eyes, now, Livia. That's a sign of disrespect to these folks. Look down when ya speak, and if ya happen to look up at any time, don't pause there 'cause they'll think ya starin', and that's no good."

With head down, I replied, "I wouldn't think of taking the book, ma'am." *"An' remembers to keep it short and sweet-like. Answer a question and be on yer way."* I couldn't possibly keep it short after being accused a thief. "Harriet Beecher Stowe is a wonderful American writer. She captured her characters honestly and feared nothing in her conflicts. *Uncle Tom's Cabin* is a meaningful piece of literature that I was simply admiring—"

"Admiring? Ha! You are not paid to admire my father's books. What is your name?"

I looked up at the woman's face, fashionably perfect in every way with dark curls of hair dangling from beneath a tilted hat with silk roses circling the crown. A shimmering opal broach decorated the white lace creeping up her neck, and her pink lips matched the rich mauve shawl draped upon her shoulders.

"Livia. Livia Haas."

"And from where do you get your education, Miss Livia?"

I returned my gaze downward. "I learned to read back in Pennsylvania, ma'am, and I've been educating myself most of the time since."

"I assumed you had no formal schooling. Schools teach manners and work ethic."

"Sincerely, ma'am. I am an honest and hard worker. I promise not to let myself get side-tracked again." Sweat was forming on my brow, and my whole body shook with dread.

"I won't report this incident, but rest assured I'll be watching out for you, Livia Haas."

She moved toward the door as I retrieved the dust rag, pushing back tears.

"Have you anything to say about Whitman?" she asked, turning back.

"He is a master. An inspiration," I responded.

"If you're as honest as you say, you'll respect my father and his love for literature by keeping things in order."

"Yes, ma'am."

"Do you clean?"

"Of course, I do! You can check the parlors with a white glove, and I dare you to find any dust!" This time I couldn't help but look her in eye.

"You *dare* me?"

"I didn't mean it like that." *This is why I should keep things short!*

"Hmm." She left as Clementine entered.

"What were you doin', girl, talkin' to a Sherman?" Clementine asked in a hurried whisper.

"Oh, Clem, she accused me of stealing a book!"

"Lord have mercy, child! What did you say?"

"I think I'm safe. She said she wouldn't report me, but I'm

shaking."

She grabbed the rag from me. "What in the world are you still doin' here anyways?"

"What time is it?" I questioned.

"Jus' 'bout half past six, girl."

"Oh my! And I have yet to beat the rugs. I apologize if you've had to stay late on my account?"

"Girl, I'm here to nearly 8:00 every night, an' that has nothin' to do with you, but poor Willie's probably been waitin' 'round fer over half an hours by nows."

"Waiting? Will has been waiting? Where?" I looked about.

"Didn't ya read the note?"

"No! Oh, no, I got engrossed with this library, and I completely forgot!"

Dearest Livia,

I'll be caught up all day but would like the opportunity to escort you home this evening. I can meet you outside at the corner of Randolph and Clark. We can chat leisurely on the horse-car, and don't worry about the nickel; the fare is my treat. I look forward to seeing you again. I shall wait for you at 6:00.

Sincerely,

Will

"I see him still out theres," Clementine reported from behind the curtain. "Now git goin' 'fore he leaves all broken hearted."

"But what about the rugs?"

"I'll cover it for ya, and if I sees Martha Sherman, I'll take care of things. Now jus' git." Clementine gave me a little push.

"I owe you for this, Clementine," I said while untying my apron. "I owe you for a lot of things."

I was frantic as I hurried back to the kitchen changing room and replaced my uniform with my street clothes and dashed out the door. Will was nowhere to be seen. I turned in circles and tried my best to spy his features in the twilight hues of the evening. "Will!" I called out. "Will!" I heard no response, but I felt the passersby staring at me, and then they were snickering to each other. Afraid to cause a scene for the Sherman patrons to hear or see, I refrained from further calls. I crossed the street and sat on a bench in front of the courthouse, making eye contact with each person who walked along, but not one of them was Will. He was gone. He had left. He was probably just as miserable. I waited still as the bells began to ring their seven sounds. An opportunity lost, and it was my entire fault. He had already gone to great lengths on several occasions, and I hadn't had the courtesy of being prompt. *How stupid! Why didn't I read his letter at lunch? I had thought of him at every lunch break since I started, but today, thoughts of Will were replaced with thoughts of literature! And what did literature offer me?*

"Need a nickel for a ride, ma'am?"

My heart skipped a beat when I saw him looking down at me. I reacted unconsciously and hopped up to him, throwing my arms around his neck and holding him tightly. "I'm sorry." I kept saying the words over and over into his ear, and when I felt his arms wrap around my back and squeeze me closer, I knew that I was forgiven, but I could not stop the redundant apology.

Releasing my hold just enough to gaze up at Will's face, I noticed the sun readying itself to set behind him, and he seemed to glow. Instinctively I pulled him to me and kissed him on the lips. I don't know who was more stunned! I had never kissed a man, and I was not what people would describe as *forward* by any means, but it happened, and I shocked myself as well as Will.

"Well, now, with a greeting like that, isn't it enough to wait for ya every day, eh?"

"I'm so sorry, Will," I said to him, embarrassed again by my actions.

"And do you have anything else to say, or will I be forgiving ya all the way home?"

"Not about being late. I mean, at first that's what I was sorry about, but just now when I said I was sorry, I meant for throwing myself at you that way, and in public, no less, I just—" and he put his hands on my cheeks and kissed me again, softly.

"Now we're even, eh?"

The horse-car was heading in our direction; our romantic interlude came to an unwanted end. Will helped me onto the step and made a snide comment about taking my time as to not trip. I laughed. "I might make mistakes every now and again," I retorted, "but I rarely make the same one twice."

"Fair enough. Still friends?"

"And then some," I replied, and we found an empty bench.

"Did Clementine have ya working too hard today? Why so late this evening?" he asked.

"Oh, it wasn't Clementine's fault at all. It was my own

doing that I was late. First off, I hadn't read the note. After I received it, Clementine and I started talking about my new schedule for the afternoon, and when I heard that I would be in charge of cleaning Mr. Sherman's personal library, well, I almost stopped breathing for the excitement of such a thing, and when I finally walked into the room, I was dumbfounded once again by the cases, from floor to ceiling, filled with hundreds of the most amazing books you could ever find! And then his daughter came in and thought I was stealing Harriet Beacher Stowe's *Uncle Tom's Cabin*." I turned in my seat to look directly at Will, "Can you imagine? I've never been accused of anything that sinful!" He smiled as if he understood, so I continued. "Luckily, she's not reporting the incident and left just before Clementine showed up and told me the time and reminded me of my note."

"So it was a book that brought us together, and it was a *roomful* of books that nearly tore us apart. Is that what you're saying?"

"More or less, I guess you're right."

We talked about literature, mostly, all the way to my stop, and then we decided to stroll the side streets of the north side. My hand clutched the crook of his arm, pulling him close, and he spoke into me so that I could feel the warmth of his breath with every word.

"Hey, Livia."

The voice startled us, and I swung my head in the direction of the heavy accent. The deep, guttural sound was familiar but not distinct. The voice came forward again.

60

"Who's your friend?"

Will tightened his hold on my hand, and he asked me if I knew the man, but the street was dark, and I could not be certain of the face that belonged to the large figure in the shadows. I prayed it wasn't who I thought it was.

"I'm not meaning to scare you, Livia. Just wanting to make sure that this here stranger was invited to take your hand like that, or if you need a bit of assistance. You're not that type of girl, now, are ya, Liv?"

Karl was standing under the dim lamppost. Franz's army buddy squinted his eyes at Will.

Will was about to respond when I found my vocal chords. "Karl, you scared me half to death, walking out of the shadows like that. But if you must know, this is my friend and coworker, Will, who was kind enough to escort me home from a late workday."

"Will, huh?" Karl grunted. The smell of whiskey was on his breath.

"Nice to meet ya, Karl. The name is Will Magee, eh?"

He clutched my arm with his left hand, and stuck out his right to Karl. Leaving Will's hand in the air, Karl clenched his own hands into fists and asked me if Franz and my family knew about my working and getting too friendly with a "mick." My reflexes told me to pull Will away and run, but Will had his own reflexes to deal with. In a split second, Karl slapped Will's free arm down and was just about to swing an upper-cut to the jaw when Will responded with a strong punch to Karl's gut. He doubled over and fell to the ground. Will picked up his hat that had fallen to the ground next to Karl, and he whispered to the man.

"I guess ya didn't hear it right, Karl. I said it was Muh-gee, not Mick-gee. Honest mistake there, eh?"

Frightened, I took Will's arm once again, and we quickly went on our way back toward the horse-car stop. Will insisted that he walk me the entire way home, even if it meant walking on the other side of the street, so my parents or any other neighbor wouldn't take notice of him. When I entered the front door of the shop, I turned and waved and put my fingers gently on the window. He tipped his hat and kept walking along the road.

I couldn't sleep that night. My stomach was in knots with my first sense of affection for a man, and my first feeling of dread that something or someone could take him away from me. I prayed that night for our Lord to protect Will, and for my parents to receive him with favor, because this relationship had gone further than walks and talks.

CHAPTER 7

I couldn't brush off the feeling of being followed and watched. Paranoia. That's what it was. Surely, Karl wouldn't harm me. He was only being protective when seeing me with Will, right? Nonetheless, with a rosary in my pocket, I prayed all the way to work, and with a quickened pace, I arrived early at the Sherman. What a welcomed sight when I turned the corner to the back entrance.

"I'll be seeing you each morning, eh, to ensure your safe arrival. And from here out, won't I be escorting you home."

"It's unnecessary, Will. I can't ask you to spend your time and money for such an inconvenience."

"So you don't want to see me?"

"Oh, no. That's not the case at all."

"Well, no worries about the fare, Livia. My newest chairs will fetch me more than enough for our rides."

"But I'm sure you're needed elsewhere—at home, at work. I don't want to cause undue problems. How would you explain your absence each morning and evening?"

Will's hands dug deep into his trouser pockets, and he nudged the gravel ground with the toes of his boots.

"Last night, I told Ma and Da about ya, and they agreed that I should watch over my new person of interest."

My head tilted. "Person of interest?" I asked.

"Well, that's how they said it," Will replied, blushing.

"How would *you* say it?"

"What do you mean?"

"How would you describe me? My relationship with you?" Suddenly, I needed to know.

He took off his hat and ran his fingers through his hair. "You are a person, eh? And you know I'm interested in ya, but I would probably describe it a bit more intimate. Wouldn't you?"

"I would," I replied. There was silence. "What happens if Karl follows us again? I don't want to put you in danger."

"After the way I handled meself, eh? You don't have faith in me strength and wit?" He raised his arms to flex muscles hidden beneath the white sleeves of his shirt.

"I have great faith in you, Will Magee," I replied with a laugh. "I just don't like putting you in such a predicament."

"Well, then, it's settled. I'll see you this evening at the same corner, and we'll take the horse-car together."

"Will," I asked on one horse-car ride, "have you ever been accused of something that was utterly untrue?"

"Sure, Liv. In my business, customers are always trying to get something for nothing, so they accuse me of not following design details that were agreed upon, or they claim I'm overcharging for labor and materials."

"How do you deal with it? How do you respond?"

"Not much I can do, eh? Their words against mine. Unless it's all in writing, the handshake doesn't mean much anymore."

The horse-car came to an abrupt halt causing our bodies to slide on the wooden bench. Will's leg touched mine, but instead of readjusting ourselves, we remained close as he put an arm around me.

"What's rufflin' your feathers, Liv? Sherman's daughter thought you were stealing again, eh?"

"No, but that's when the accusations started. It just seems that I've been misunderstood lately, and it bothers me."

"Well, if it's not Martha Sherman, then who else?"

"There's a delightful family living at the Sherman House, the Gages. Have you heard of them?"

"The city treasurer?"

"That's the one. His name is Mr. David Gage, and he lives at the hotel with his wife and brother. He also has a daughter Clara who's married to Robert Clarke, and the young couple comes to visit from time to time."

He nodded.

"Well, this afternoon, Mr. and Mrs. Gage were hosting Mr. and Mrs. Clarke for lunch. I was summoned to their suite to clean up a spill of red wine, and I quickly brought my solution of water, vinegar, and soap. The foursome was out on the terrace, so I poured the solution on the stain in the parlor and left it to soak. I returned just five minutes later, only to find Mrs. Clarke moaning and regurgitating into a pot in the powder room."

"And you were accused of causing the sickness?"

"I was accused of being insensitive to the heightened smells of a pregnant woman."

"That's a bit extreme, now wouldn't ya say, Liv."

"Nothing is extreme when talking about a woman with child, Will, but I didn't *know* Mrs. Clarke was pregnant. Had I been aware of the fact, I would have blotted the best I could with water and soap and waited on the vinegar solution until after she left. I witnessed what Catherine went through during the first half of her pregnancy, the nausea and discomfort and sickness. I am not insensitive."

"No need to try to convince me." He rubbed his thumb along my shoulder, and I hoped he didn't notice the goose-bump quiver it caused. "Tell me how things turned out."

"Even after my explanation and apologies, the Gages no longer want me to service their suite. They've requested a different servant."

Will pulled me closer. I tightened the clasp of my folded hands on my lap, unsure of what to do.

"Aw, Liv. Don't let it get to ya."

"It's hard not to when that was just another accusation added to the list this week." I used my finger as an imaginary pen and pretended to jot down the list on my palm. "I am a thief; I am insensitive; I am inept because Mr. Rutherford's ice water didn't have enough ice; I am selfish because I could not cover an overnight shift for a coworker; I am a cheat because Mrs. Caufield's fruit bowl had two less pieces than Mrs. Brown's fruit bowl. Shall I go on?"

"Won't I go on for you." He removed his arm from around me, took my palm and used his own forefinger to write. "You are beautiful, ya see. You are intelligent. You are diligent and conscientious and loyal." Will stopped "writing." "Now, which accusations are more accurate, eh?"

"I should hope, yours."

"Well, our Lord blessed the world when you entered it, Livia Haas, and you shouldn't pay any mind to those who don't know you and don't appreciate the gift you are."

"Our Lord? You almost sounded religious."

He let go of my palm, returning his hands to his own knees, and I restrained myself from exhaling a disappointed sigh.

"I may not be religious, but I have been baptized."

"You're Catholic, then?"

"Me ma's as devout a Catholic as they come, attending daily Mass and praying for my soul with every rosary she recites. Now St. Gerard is her favorite saint for bringing six healthy children into this world, but isn't it St. Joseph on whom she most depends with a husband and sons as carpenters, eh?"

"I'm dumbfounded."

"Why so?"

"I never thought you were Catholic, Will. I don't know why. Maybe it's because you're Irish, and most of the Irish people I've met or heard about have been Protestant."

"For someone who's disturbed by accusations, Miss Haas, I'm surprised, eh, that you could have such a biased thought based on my ethnicity." He used a sarcastic tone, but I agreed with him. Will was right, and I didn't attempt to make excuses.

"Coming from anyone else, I might get defensive with such an honest declaration of my faults, but you're correct, Will Magee. I was being judgmental, and I shouldn't have. What's more is the fact that I'm delighted in this new knowledge."

CHAPTER 8

Catherine wasn't due for another two months, but her heart had been racing in recent days. Franz ordered her to bed rest, and Father ordered me to go back to rolling and wrapping and packing the cigars every morning. Catherine felt awful foisting her responsibilities on me, so I took on the chores with a smile and did all that was required with no fuss or sign of exhaustion. It was miserable work at such an early hour, long before daybreak when the moon was still in plain sight, but I was determined to keep my spirits up for Catherine's sake. Clementine was my role model, as I witnessed her toiling from sun up to sundown without a single yawn or sigh to signal fatigue. Adding to my long days were the heat and drought. I hadn't remembered the temperature this warm for the end of September, nor did I recall when our last rain had come. The unusual weather was taking its toll on local crops, so when Mother went to market, much of the fruits and vegetables and grains we didn't grow in our own backyard, were of poorer quality. At least Father was grateful that the tobacco farms back in Pennsylvania were not experiencing the same fate; Franz went to the station each Monday for our newly delivered supply of leaves, and all seemed fresh. Even so, times were tough.

And then there was Will, the bright spot of every day while he was working at the Sherman. As long as I was dismissed on time, we could take a walk and then hop on the horse-car, and when I got home no one wondered why I was a few minutes or half hour tardy, since there was never a scheduled time for my return to begin with. Some days there'd be late deliveries to be made, but Franz did me that favor after I started doing Catherine's work, and I was thankful.

"How are you feeling?" I whispered to my friend as I tiptoed into her room, not wanting to wake Junior asleep on the cot on the floor.

"Ridiculously fine. I should not be held up in this bed, Livia," Catherine replied as she set her sewing material down on the night stand between her and her son.

"You have better coloring in your face."

"That's what I'm saying. We're truly all right," she said massaging her belly. I scooted beside her and laid back to share the pillow behind our backs. "And even though I enjoy reading and sewing, I am finding both pleasantries a complete bore, so please, PLEASE, tell me you've got some stories to share."

"I might have a story or two for you," I said with a grin.

"Do tell, do tell."

"He wants me to come to dinner to meet his family," I blurted.

"When?" Catherine couldn't believe her ears.

"I told Will that a Saturday would work best. Maybe next Saturday, or the following."

"I think it's time for the Haas family to meet Will, too. If you're going to meet the Magees, why wait with your own parents, Liv?"

Junior wrestled under his covers, and I placed a finger to my lips.

I whispered. "Mother and Father will side with Franz, who

69

will surely frown upon my choice in men once your husband finds out about what Will did to Karl."

"I'm missing something, Liv. How does Will know Karl?"

I explained to Catherine about the altercation, and I told her about Will escorting me home every night since.

"I don't know why Franz keeps treating Karl like his hero. I wish I knew what actually happened when Karl "saved" my husband. I understand brotherly ties were made during the war, but I, like you, feel apprehensive when it comes to Karl. He's just, well...manipulative."

Catherine took a deep breath with pursed lips and flaring nostrils, and that expression was the only indication of anger that came from my even tempered friend. On exhale, she continued.

"It still appalls me to think of Franz being guilted into going out with that man when he was supposed to be spending time with Junior last Saturday. Karl told him to meet at Turner, and Franz replied that he'd have to be late, and do you know what that so-called hero said?" She folded her arms across her chest as I shook my head *no*. "He said, 'Well, my brother, I'm not one for waiting, as I proved on the battlefield when I saved you.'"

"That's awful," I agreed.

"I don't trust him," Catherine concluded. "Intoxication is no excuse for attacking Will. Karl is a strange one, and Franz doesn't see it."

"I know, Catherine. That's why I didn't confide in you until now. I'll have to tell the family about this Karl incident if I'm going to bring Will around. What should I do?"

"He's Catholic."

"Yes."

"There you go."

"What do you mean?"

"Karl isn't Catholic, Livia. Since your parents already know how you feel about Karl's odd behavior, and if you tell them what happened that night, and if they understand that Will protected you, that *Catholic* Will protected you, I don't think you have any problem here."

"It's not about Karl versus Will. I think it's more like Franz versus Will. When Karl tells your husband about that night, he'll make up some kind of story to avoid making himself look bad. I know it. Franz is going to hate Will before he even meets him. And if Franz hates Will, my parents won't give him a chance."

"I'll handle Franz," said Catherine reassuringly. Then she turned away and added, "It's about time we have a sit-down Karl-talk anyway."

"You just changed your expression to one of worry. Has he been having nightmares again?" I asked, and she nodded.

I, myself, had heard Franz's cries in the dark of night, but Catherine wouldn't come to me to talk about it, not anymore, not since the last time we talked about Franz's dream terrors back in Quakertown. We were picking tomatoes from our abundant garden, and that encounter marked the saddest day of my life.

"Bad night?"

"Three in a row. He wakes in such heavy sweats, the linens are soaked through, and if he's not grabbing his leg screaming in imaginary pain, he's sitting up with a dream dagger piercing the darkness. He's never harmed me, but I'm in fear most nights,

71

that unintentionally he could, that in the midst of his nightmares I might not roll away quick enough." She went on. "He weeps in his sleep, and just now he was humming the melody to that somber song, 'The Vacant Chair.'"

"You must get some rest, Catherine. What can I do for you?"

"It's not me for which something needs to be done; it's Franz. I'm at a loss as to how to help him, Liv."

"Do you think he might need to see a doctor? He's surely not the only one with these nagging memories."

"He refuses and says a shot of whiskey before bed is the best cure. Sometimes that helps, but other times I think it aggravates his condition." She took a deep breath. "What's worse is that army buddy, Karl, is writing again. Franz received another note just yesterday begging him to move to Chicago for a change of scenery."

"Oh, Catherine, you're not thinking of leaving us, are you? I couldn't bear it!" I exclaimed.

"The man wants all of us to come. It's odd. Franz must have spoken to Karl about everyone at great length, because each letter mentions the whole Haas family. Some notes inquire more about your parents' well being than Junior's and mine."

"But we couldn't just up and leave with Jonas away."

"Of course not, Livia. I shouldn't have mentioned it."

"But you did, and I can't help but wonder if this has been brought up with anyone else."

"Franz has talked to your parents, and they responded the same as us. We can't discuss a move before Jonas returns."

"I think Father might consider it, though, with Uncle George being buried some place out there. He's always wanted more information."

"Otto wrote to Jonas, and your brother gave his blessing, but it just doesn't feel right, at least not now, and anyway, I'm not sure I want Junior being raised in the city. Farm life is all I know; it's all any of us has ever known." Catherine rubbed her eyes. "And there's another thing. It's silly, but just the same —"

"What, Catherine?" She was too quiet for my liking.

"Lord, forgive me for thinking that this Karl has sinister intentions, but I can't help myself. Livia, Franz has absolutely no recollection of the shooting incident. He remembers all the battles, more than he wants, but he says he blacked out and remembers nothing about Karl's rescue. My husband depends entirely on this stranger's stories to fill in the blanks."

"Wouldn't that be understandable, though? I mean with shock and all, maybe the worst gets hidden, or maybe Franz was unconscious," I said.

"I guess, but what concerns me most is Franz's nightmares about Karl's hands being covered in blood. Franz tells me how he desperately attempts to help him, but no matter how hard he scrubs, the blood continues to drip, and Karl doesn't mind. The dream is bothersome. To my husband, it's unfair to not feel connected to Karl the way Karl feels connected to Franz."

"Franz has been through a lot, Catherine. Pray for patience, my friend," I replied.

Catherine smiled and held out her hand to assist me to my feet. It was then that we heard a horse-cart trotting down the road.

By the time we got to the house, I saw Father running toward the barn; the front door was wide open. Franz was on the porch leaning over the bannister with dry heaves, his face reddened and wet. Catherine handed me her basket and flew to her husband's side while I rushed into the house to get cool rags.

"What has happened?" I said, finding my mother in the kitchen mumbling in her German tongue, her body crumpled across the table, her hands white from squeezing the rosary beads that were part clenched in her fist and part laying on top of a piece of paper. It was a letter addressed to The Parents of Jonas Haas from the United States Army.

WE REGRET TO INFORM YOU...

"No!" I screamed. "No!"

Catherine massaged her unborn child. "Yes, there have been recurring dreams, but don't fret. I'll talk to Franz and set things right."

"Don't say anything just yet, Catherine. I'm the one who should address him. I just need to figure out the best time and approach." I leaned my head on Catherine's shoulder. "I don't know what I'd do without you. You're like the sister I never had."

"Likewise, Livia. You're a sister-dream come true."

"Hopefully you've had bigger dreams than simply wanting a sibling."

"Sure, I've dreamt of writing or teaching, but university was never an option after my parents died, and then I met Franz, and I formed new dreams of being a wife and mother, and here I am." She gave her stomach a gentle hug. "I'm very content with the way things have turned out."

"I've dreamed the same dreams, you know?" I told her.

"Really?"

"Yes, really. Before bed each night, no matter how tired I am, I write several pages in my journal because I promised Jonas that I'd write and pray, always. Lately, the pages are mostly about Will, but I keep thinking that someday I might uncover a little seed of a story to create, and then when I'm helping Junior with his studies, especially with his literature and rhetoric, I often dream of being a teacher, too."

"You could do it, Livia," Catherine told me as she sat up straight.

"No, I couldn't."

"Yes, Livia. It's not too late for you. You have a job. You could start saving your money for university. I don't make much as a seamstress, but I could save some, too. You could get that degree for both of us." The sparkle in Catherine's eyes was bright and shining in the glow of her cheeks.

"And when would I have time to attend classes and do school work?" I mused.

"We'll figure it out. After the baby's born and I'm back on my feet, we'll make a plan. In the meantime, you need to start thinking about what you'll wear when meeting the Magees."

CHAPTER 9

He was waiting for me at the usual corner, and I smiled from ear to ear. We headed toward the lakefront where families and couples were already enjoying the pleasant early evening, barefoot and strolling along the shoreline, letting their toes dig deep into the sand.

Will took off his jacket and laid it on the beach. He smiled and signaled with open palms for me to be seated. I did so, but not before I caught a glimpse of his broad shoulders. I gathered my skirt on my lap and relaxed, gazing out at the water's reflection of the setting sun behind us. "Serenity," I sighed.

"Do ya mind if I sit with ya?" asked Will.

"Of course not."

He stood behind me and then sat with a leg on either side of my body. His arms came round my waist, and before I knew it I was snuggled close upon his chest. His heart was beating fast.

"I've got us some tickets to the opera, eh," he said.

I turned my head toward him. Our faces were close enough to touch, but I felt the lake breeze saunter through the gap between my lips and his cheek.

"Tickets? To the Crosby Opera House? For you and me?"

He stared out at the water, an approving look upon his face.

"For Thursday. I've never been, but I'd like to go with ya, if you'll accept the invitation that is."

"Of course, I'll go to the opera with you!" I nestled back on his body. "I don't think I've been happier than this moment right now. Even my headache seems to be relieved."

I felt Will's chin rest on my shoulder. He let his head tilt to touch mine, and my insides quivered.

"Meet me again tomorrow morning?" he whispered. The words were like poetry singing off the waves of the lake. I deliberated and then declined.

"Tomorrow's Sunday, Will. On Sundays my family breakfasts together, and then our Mass is always quite long. Don't you do the same?"

"Ah, well certainly I eat breakfast, Liv."

"And church?"

"Me ma and sisters attend, but I guess us men, with no disrespect to the household women, have a few issues, eh?"

I paused and sat forward, breaking the enclosed circle of his arms. I twisted my body to face him. "Issues?" I asked. "What kind of issues would cause your absence from church? You are Catholic, right?"

"Yes, Liv. I was baptized a Catholic, and I don't intend to lie to ya. I do believe strongly in God, but isn't religion another matter."

"Another matter? How does one separate God from religion?"

"Well, sometimes I think religions, including Catholicism, are simply man's creation. One group takes their interpretation of God and creates laws and doctrines and truths to support their interpretation, and those they can convince of its authenticity become the followers."

"So Jesus was just a man with an interpretation? That's what you believe?"

"Now, why are we having this conversation, Liv?"

"Because it's important, Will. We've talked before about my family, about my being a practicing Catholic, and yet you asked me to skip a sacred day of the church, so now I'm asking you to explain your apathy toward religion."

The intimacy shared just minutes earlier had shattered into pieces of tension.

"I said I believe in God, okay Liv? I also believe in the existence of Jesus, and as a matter-of-fact, I respect any man who can rebel against evil, rally the common people, and together fight for a better world."

"And what about the Bible?"

"C'mon Liv, must we continue this?"

"Yes, we must." There was a brief silence, and I could see that Will was flustered with me, so I added, "I'm not angry with you, Will, but I'm trying to understand your position, and I think I have a right to that understanding if we're to continue seeing each other." The silence lingered. I pressed on. "So, the Bible?"

"So, the Bible." No longer embracing me, Will leaned back, his arms now behind him, bracing his weight. "To me, the Bible is a beautiful and compelling piece of literature, it is, and though each story of the Old Testament has incredible moral merit, and the New Testament includes moving biographies of Jesus' life, I believe the authors to be hand picked to support the views of a specific religion. Yes, I question the book as a work of pure facts, as an authentic know-all account, which can be regarded above and beyond any other religious Holy Book such as the

Torah or Koran."

"So you have no faith in Christianity?"

He scooted away from me, just an inch or two, but distant enough to show a divide.

"Well now, faith demands followers to believe whole-heartedly, to obey without question, to practice without reservation, eh. But when one's faith is used as a basis for war and persecution, as is the case in Ireland where my relatives are tormented for their Catholic principles; when faith is used as an excuse to keep down the down-trodden, as it does each day when the employers in Packingtown take wages away from the poor, explaining that the employees' sacrifices will help build a library or park for the betterment of society; when the wealthy and religious establishment sacrifices nothing in return, at these times and many others, now, don't I find religion to be hypocritical and blind faith to be ignorant."

"Ignorant," I repeated. "Hmm."

"Not you, Liv."

This time it was me who pulled away.

"Right. Only those who fail to question are ignorant."

"Yes."

"But Will, isn't that what faith is all about? I mean, sure I question literature, I question rules, I question many things, but when it comes to religion, belief without proof is what faith means."

"Sure, but—"

"So according to your rant, any faithful member of any religion is ignorant, which means you have now labeled me, as a practicing Catholic, as ignorant."

"Liv—"

"And to think that I've been fooling myself all of these years, pretending to be somewhat intellectual." I straightened my spine and stood to shake the sand from my clothes and added, "Thank you, Mr. Magee, for enlightening me. I guess I need to come to grips with my true ignorant self."

"You can twist me words as much as ya like, but people don't have to compromise their faith in God by questioning the men who have blessed themselves as the authority." The couple nearest us looked in our direction, but Will continued. "When people simply follow rules for the sake of law, whether it be political or religious, eh, and when people fail to question the decision making that is done *for* them instead of *by* them, and when corruption runs rampant through its leadership without so much as a simple "why?" from the people, I call it ignorance, I do." He reached for his jacket and started slapping it clean. "I don't condone defiance toward God, ya see, but won't I forever encourage the questioning of mere men."

At the completion of his monologue, he was still sitting in the sand, his elbows on his knees and hands folded in the space where I had been. Frustrated but sincere in his convictions, Will had experiences I never had, knowledge of things I did not comprehend, and a passion far deeper than anyone I had ever met. I knelt by his side and ran my fingers through his dampened hair. "Come to Mass with me tomorrow," I said quietly.

"Pardon?" he retorted while swinging his reddened face

around so quickly I thought his neck might snap. "Have you listened to anything I've said?" Confusion was written in the creases of his forehead, in the squint of his eyes, in the pursing of his lips.

"Yes, of course I've been listening, and quite frankly, you make valid points that pertain to the weaknesses of leadership while failing to admit the positive influence of spirit, the positive influence that the majority of faithful have on creating a better world."

He looked away. "No thanks, Liv. I'm sorry, but no."

"Think about it, Will. Seriously. You wouldn't even have to hear a single word of scripture or preaching because the entire Mass is said in Latin, and the hymns are sung in German."

Turning back to me, he couldn't help but grin. "So you want me to go to church to prove *what*, may I ask?"

"Not to prove anything, just to share the spirit of it with you." There was an awkward pause. "Will, it's admirable to be an independent thinker, but it is also reassuring and rewarding to be part of a flock, to be surrounded by the power of good people struggling in the same world with the same good intentions."

He shook his head in disbelief, looked up at me with a smirk and said, "You want me to be a sheep, eh?"

It was something Jonas would have said to me, and I laughed out loud. "You don't give up, Will Magee, do you? Would it be more appropriate to ask you to be a part of a herd instead of flock? Let's say, a herd of mules, maybe?"

He took me in his arms again, turned my body over his, and then placed me on the ground where he laid at my side.

"Are ya saying ya still love me?" he asked.

"Still? Hmm. Well that's a bit presumptuous, *eh*?"

"Now aren't I just hoping that, even after a discussion as tense as this, I can presume reciprocation of my feelings." He touched my cheek with his thumb.

"You can't say it directly, can you?"

"Say what?"

"Tell me, Will."

His smile was that of a little boy with his fair skin blushing bright pink, and then he gave me a soft kiss. "I love ya, Livia Haas, I do," he whispered. "I've never said that to a woman before, but haven't I ever felt this strongly before, either." I put my arms around his neck without a care of passersby.

"I love you, too, Will."

CHAPTER 10

From a mile away I could see its steeple towering over the neighborhood, a constant reminder that the Lord's house was forever in our midst, and as we approached the entrance doors on Cleveland Avenue, tall and wide, anyone who entered couldn't help but feel like a princess or prince arriving at the palace of our King. For an hour or more each Sunday, I found hope in the hymns, peace in the prayers, and most times, the sermons hugged me with a spiritual embrace.

This is what I wanted for Will. If Mother had known about his doubt and denial of our faith, she would have prayed a novena for his soul, but personally, I cared more about our life here on earth. I believed we were meant to meet; I believed in divine intervention.

The steeple bells were still chiming when we rose for the processional song. Mother was on my right nearest Father at the aisle, while Catherine was on my left with Junior sandwiched between his parents, already fidgeting in his youthful anticipation of the upcoming service.

The monsignor approached his chair; the final note of the choir's harmony hit when I noticed him— and gasped out loud. Mother's eye of disgrace fell in my direction. I felt the heads of everyone around us turn toward me, and I quickly whispered, "a hiccup."

It took all the self-control I could muster to avoid looking in his direction until such a peek could come at a natural moment. Five minutes seemed like an eternity, but when I saw him again

—the waves in the back of his hair, the wide and muscular line across his shoulders, the distinct protrusion of his jaw—I immediately thanked God for bringing him to this place.

This Sunday was the only time I found myself unfocused at Mass. But what could one expect? Will Magee had accepted the invitation.

I did not witness his exit, but I assumed his departure took place at communion time, leaving out the side door so as to not bring attention to his forgoing the host and wine. It would have been inappropriate to take the Eucharist, and I respected him for respecting the Mass.

As the bells rang out, our family made small talk with other parishioners on the church steps, when I was pushed aside by several hurried young men who ran quickly down the avenue and carelessly across the street. *They'll be hit by the next carriage if they carry on that way.* My eyes followed the group as it made its way toward a gentleman leaning against an old elm tree. Each boy took turns speaking, got patted on the head, and then handed something, something small that fit the palm of each hand. *A coin?* The man watched the last child, one similar in size to Junior and wearing a faded forage cap, run off. The man looked back at St. Michael's. I recognized that suspicious snarl.

Will was not waiting for me at the back entrance on Monday morning, but Clementine was.

"I should be a paid messenger with all these notes I be passin'," said Clementine as she handed me an envelope. "The

Shermans are outta town nows, so I'm guessin' it'd be all right to read it whenever you like."

I promptly ripped open the letter and read it out loud.

My Dearest Liv,

Doesn't it seem I'm feeling a bit under the weather. I won't be working today, and I (regretfully) won't be around for our northerly journey. I'm enclosing a nickel for your fare. Please take the horse-car, and do be cautious. I worry about your being alone these days. Be safe, my angel. I promise to see you soon.

Love,

Will

P.S. I think you may be right about some things.

"Something has happened, Clem."

"Now what makes you say that?" she asked.

"I know it. Will wouldn't skip work. He wouldn't skip seeing me, not today, not when he knows how I've been dying to talk to him since yesterday."

"And what happened yesterday?"

"Will went to Mass at my church. I wasn't able to speak with him, but I saw him."

"Well, good for you, Livia, bringing some God-fearin' love back to that boy's life again."

"No, Clem. It should have been good, but it wasn't." I told Clementine about Karl and about my instinct that he may have had Will followed. My mind started racing, and my body shook.

"And you thinks Karl found him?"

"Yes, I do." I sat on a stool near the kitchen counter and buried my face in my hands.

"Come, come now, girl. Will's a strong man. Real strong. He knew how to take care of hisself the first time they met, so what makes you think he couldn't take care of hisself if Karl met up with him a second time?"

"Karl was looking for revenge, Clem." Her brows lifted above wide eyes, identifying her own nervousness. "How did you get this envelope?"

"It was attached to the back door when I came in. He must have put it there sometime between ten last night when I left and five this mornin' when I arrived."

"Do you know Will's address, Clem?"

"The only thing I knows about his family home is that this hotel is between it and the carpentry business. I can't tell you how many times I gets to work here and find a note or a bag of them peaches from his backyard, an' when I'm thankin' him, Will always tells me its no problem at all 'cause the Sherman is right on his way to work."

The shop was not too far a distance.

"Just git on with ya, Liv. If anyone asks, I'll tell 'em that you're delayed. And if you see him, tell Will I'm prayin' for him."

"Thanks Clem. You're a true friend."

I hurried out the back and made a mad dash eastward on Lake Street, almost as far as I could go where the railroad tracks fenced off Lake Michigan. The business district and shopping areas slowly disappeared with every block by which I passed. A single corner turn brought into view a row of clapboard structures with narrow passageways between them and simple hand chiseled signs above the doorways marking the type of trade dwelled within. As sensitive as my nose could be, the aroma of coal and smoke from the trains on the adjacent rails proved secondary to the new ringing and echoing in my ears and head as these city lifelines screeched and roared minute by minute.

The sign read MAGEE FAMILY CARPENTRY, all letters in perfect symmetry, and the front windows were shuttered. I knocked several times with no response, so I walked around to the rear. Peach trees and a full garden filled the small space, and wooden shavings were layered thick along the planked walkway lining the wall. I knocked at the back door and peered in the only uncovered window, but no one was in sight. I waited.

It wasn't long before I heard a tapping sound coming from the alley. A man with a walking cane was now standing on the property. He was short in stature with an elongated face and pronounced cheek bones behind the stubble of a beard not yet fully grown in. As he approached, I noticed the similar hint of gray in his eyes.

"If you're not Livia, won't I have a lot of explaining to do to the missus," he said.

"I am. Are you Will's father?" I asked.

"I am proud to confirm with a 'yes'," replied Mr. Magee, and he motioned for me to sit down on one of the benches beneath the tree.

"Something bad happened to Will, didn't it Mr. Magee?"

"If ya think being clubbed from behind and clobbered in the eye as bad, well, then, I guess you are correct, now aren't ya, Miss Livia."

"Oh, my Lord, is he okay?" The tears began to form. "I must see him."

"He's in some pain, he is, but dear, it could have been much worse, eh? The doctor says that the jaw's not broke, but it will be a while before the swelling comes down around the eye. There was a concussion, of course, but aren't Mrs. Magee and I taking good care of him."

I couldn't speak.

"He's going to be fine, Livia," he said, patting my shoulder.

"Can I see him?" I asked.

"The doctor gave Will some medicine to make him sleepy, so he wouldn't have to feel all the pain while he's healin'. I'd wait a day or so, Livia, but wouldn't a visit be the thing to brighten his mood."

"Wednesday, then." It sounded a lifetime away. "Will you tell him that I'm sorry, Mr. Magee?"

"No need to be sorry, dear. And wasn't my son right?"

"Right about what, sir?"

"Right about finding the perfect lady with the purest and kindest of souls. He said you'd come lookin' for him, he did." He rose from the bench. "Come. Step inside the shop, now, and I'll write down the directions to our home."

CHAPTER 11

Clementine tried her best to get me out as quickly as possible, and she packed a bag of fresh breads she had baked for the Magees and several scarves she had knitted for the upcoming winter season.

"No knowin' when the cold snap is gonna begin in this city. Just give these here scarves to Mrs. Magee and tell her to use 'em for whoevers needs 'em."

"Thanks, Clem." I took the bag and practically tripped out the door.

There was a pronounced change in scenery from the business district—its bold buildings, tidied walkways and landscaped lawns, the frills and top hats of the passersby—to the South district where the community of scattered farmhouses, dilapidated barns, and muck-filled alleyways, struggled to thrive with little industry, except for a small drug store and several run-down saloons. The Magee home was over the Chicago River, over the trench of sewage and garbage, and I cupped my handkerchief over my mouth as I made my way toward Clinton Avenue.

Maybe it was mind over matter or just plain wishful thinking, but I was glad that the stink evaporated when I approached the 800 block, right down the road from St. Paul Church. Nothing luxurious or fancy, the rickety house was well kept and adorned with wooden benches under a shade tree in the front yard. I noticed etched woodwork on the banisters as I stepped up to the porch. Before knocking, I took a deep breath and happened to view a set of fruit trees, further back in the side yard, surrounded by a simple garden; I wondered how it all survived on the damp and swampy earth beneath it. Even in the cloudy dusk that was approaching, the peaches seemed to sing from the branches.

The door opened before I could gather my thoughts. Mr. Magee welcomed me and showed me in to the parlor. Mismatched rosewood and mahogany chairs as well as walnut side tables crowded the center of the room, and between two small windows stood a beautifully carved oak bookshelf which housed more tools and Irish pottery than books. Will was lying on a sofa which was too long for the adjacent wall and jutted out into the archway where I entered.

A blood vessel had burst near the left pupil, creating a veil of deep red in stark contrast to the whites of Will's eyes.

"Don't be lookin' so sad, Liv." The bell-shaped bruise across the bridge of his nose widened as he grinned through the swelling. His scent was still of sawdust and wood though he hadn't seen work in days.

"I'm not as bad off as I appear, Liv. I've got all my senses about me, eh, and if it weren't for these overprotective women in the house, I'd have been back to carvin' yesterday."

"It was Karl," I stated.

"Wouldn't I remember that sound of 'mick' with every whack to my face and back. I couldn't forget that voice."

Crimson heat settled into my cheeks. Will observed my anger and warned me not to say anything for deeper fear of my safety.

"*My* safety?" I questioned. "*My* safety? Will, he needs to pay for this. What if he tries to kill you?"

"I'm not thinking that'll happen, love. He's made his point clear, and that's what he wanted to do. I'm here. I'm alive. He couldn't kill me, nor could he kill my feelings for you. We'll survive this, Liv, but not if we make matters worse, eh?"

With a full figure and straight posture, her presence was known in any room she entered. When I heard the shuffle of Mrs. Magee's shoes and turned to meet this "overprotective woman," I immediately stood respectfully without thought or hesitation. Strands of grey hair were tucked behind her ears, apparently fallen from the loose braid that ran down her back. She was holding a tray with hot tea and slices of Irish bread.

"Would you like some help, ma'am?" I asked.

"No thank you, Livia. You are our special guest, so sit yourself down and share some drink and bread with us."

"Yes, ma'am." Will moved to the couch's edge to give me space beside him.

Within minutes the small room was filled with Magees. The parents sat in two arm chairs in front of the window. Mrs. Magee sipped her tea, and Mr. Magee took small deep swallows from a glass of whiskey. I recalled my childhood when Father indulged the same way after a hard day in the field. I always wanted to try it because I enjoyed the smell of it. I had still never tasted the drink, and I wondered when Father had stopped that routine.

Sisters Anna, Evelyn, and Irene crouched on a freshly polished floor with Irene's children. The boy had to be Junior's age, and the twin girls not much older. Though polite and smiling, there was a seriousness about them. As if reading my mind, Will whispered, "They aren't pleased to have their da replaced. Irene's husband died in the war; now his brother, the kids' uncle, has moved them all into his home. Irene will marry him, of course." It was customary and sad. In an ideal world, love would follow them all. "My sister and the kids are just visiting for a few days."

While we chatted, Will's sisters shared silly memories of sibling pranks they'd played on one another in their youthful days. One particular story reminded me of my own relationship with Jonas, when I had found a wonderful hiding spot, sure to fool my brother.

"I waited so long in the pantry, hidden beneath smelly linens in a laundry basket, that I fell asleep," I explained. "Unbeknownst to me, however, Jonas had only pretended to seek me out before going to town with our father, and when they returned two hours later, all the farm hands were yelling my name in the fields."

Will's nieces and nephew giggled at the details.

"What happened?" the twins asked.

"Did you wake up and come out, or did someone find you?" asked the boy.

"Well, a somber Jonas said he had peeked while counting and knew where I had hid, so he led our frantic mother, rosary beads tangled through her fingers, to the pantry. He even told me later that he chuckled to himself while in town, thinking of me coming out and whining about his unfairness in the game.

But it was me who got the last laugh because Jonas' punishment was to do my chores for a whole week!"

The girls came closer to me. "Tell us another story," they begged. "Or play a game with us!"

"Do you have any jacks?" I asked.

The trio looked up at their mother with hopeful eyes.

"In the drawer," Irene said, pointing to the sideboard, and both girls ran simultaneously to see who could find them first.

Ducking his way through the doorway, Charles Magee walked in the parlor and immediately grabbed the boy and held him high in the air until he yelled out through howling laughter, "I give up! I give up!" The girls instantly forgot about the jacks and attacked Charles' legs until they had wrestled the man to the ground and sat upon him. "Do you give up, Uncle Charlie? Do you give up?" they cried as they tried to tickle him. "I do! I give up!" he called out, and finally all the room was giggling at the children's joy.

Will cleared his throat. When Charlie looked in his direction, he noticed me.

"Well, well, would this be Harriet, Abigail, or Livia? I get confused with all the female callers for my dear brother." Mrs. Magee rose to her feet, slapping Charlie's arm for the comment and taking his coat.

"Thanks, Ma," he said, and then he turned to shake my hand. "Aren't I teasing. There's surely no other than you, Miss Livia, and isn't it a pleasure to finally meet your acquaintance."

"It's a pleasure to meet you, too, Charlie. And your entire family at that, but I'm afraid I need to start on my way home." I turned to Will. "I really do need to get going."

Mr. Magee rose from his chair. "I'll walk you to the horse-car stop."

"That isn't necessary, Mr. Magee," I said.

"Yes, it is," Will replied, and he struggled to his feet.

"When will I see you again?" I asked.

"Won't I see ya tomorrow, of course. Try your best to get out of the Sherman on time, eh, so we won't be late."

"Late? For what?"

"The opera, Liv. You didn't forget about the opera, did ya?"

"It's not that I forgot, Will, but under the circumstances, I think it best to postpone our date. Wouldn't you say so, too?

"No, I wouldn't say so at all, eh. It'll do me good to get out of the house, especially if I'm escorting the beautiful Livia Haas." He paused and then touched his cheekbone tenderly. "Are you embarrassed to be seen on my arm when I've still got bruises on me face?"

"Absolutely not!" I smiled. The flirtatious one. "Not many men can sport black and blue like you."

CHAPTER 12

"Come on outta there, will ya, girl. I swear you movin'
slower than molasses, and Willie's gonna be held up again. No
knowin' when he'll get tired of waitin' on ya."

As I stepped out, it was dim in the corridor, but even without
natural sunlight, the details of the dress were visible. "Angel
wheat" is what I had called it when Catherine took the gown
from the cedar chest, the cotton flouncing in the air like the
waves and color of grain meadows. It was her wedding dress,
and though I had refused her offer several times, she started
tailoring it straight away. Lavender satin ribbons she weaved
through the simple scalloped lace that accentuated a revealing
deep V neckline.

"Whoo-eee, Livia! Don't you look like heaven itself!"

"Really, Clem? It's not too plunging?" I asked, trying to
adjust the shoulders to pull up the cleavage point.

"Ha!" she exclaimed, slapping my hand away. "Leave it
alone, Liv. You looks like you stepped right from a dream, girl.
Only problem I see is that poor Willie's gonna be fightin' back
his eyes from starin' at ya, is all. And that ain't no bad thing."

"Well, I've never worn anything quite like this before. I feel
naked."

"That's because your neck is bare. Ya gotta let some of that
hair down." Clementine stepped around my back and
unloosened my bun. "Speakin' of molasses, that's the shade of
these, here, locks. Ain't it a shame you gotta wear this all up so
tight." Her hands worked their way through the length and

thickness, and a smaller bun was refastened. I felt loose strands hanging about my neck and framing my face.

"One more thing," she said and pulled an orchid from a vase. "The lilac color matches the ribbon and adds a soft scent."

After poking the back of my hair with floral sprigs, she stepped back for a final look.

"Now, walk back and forth a little, so I can sees the whole picture."

I strolled shakily past the counters and chopping blocks, still cluttered with remnants from the supper hour—stacks of dirty plates and pans, a bowl of trimmed meat fat waiting to be rendered, a pot of leftover stewed apples ready for preserving. I made a semi-sophisticated turn on my heels with head high, elbows touching my sides while palmed-up hands raised as if in praise. Unfortunately, I tripped but caught myself before knocking over an empty bucket.

"Watch yourself, Liv," Clem called out. "Whys you walkin' like that? Just be yourself instead of a fashion queen."

"I'm wearing Catherine's old but hardly worn boots, and she's a bit smaller in size."

"Well, that can't be comfortable. Let me have a look."

I sat on a stool and lifted the floor length gown to show the ankle high shoe.

"That toe's too narrow. Untie 'em and let me works it out some." She used a small hammer to stretch the material, and within minutes the boots were a custom fit for my feet.

"I don't know what I'd do without you, Clem," I said, still sitting on the stool and admiring the fit and feel.

"I knows what you'd do. You'd be late for every moment of your life, includin' this opera date with Willie."

"It's time, isn't it?" A flutter stirred in my stomach.

"Yes, siree, Livia. It's time." She took my hand and gave it a pat. "Now goes and have yourself a good time."

I spied him, a saluting hand held up to block the sunset, searching for me down the street. Walking slowly and carefully, I let my arms swing slightly for the breeze to catch the sheer and bell shaped sleeves, and with a deer-like stare, Will couldn't seem to divert his gaze as I approached our corner. Once in front of him, he took my fingertips and touched them like fine china. "You take my breath away," he whispered. I noticed his bashful eyes steal short glances at the lower point of my neckline, and I blushed with the pride only a woman could understand.

"Well, don't you clean up real nice, yourself, Mr. Magee."

He tipped his top-hat and bowed, offering his right elbow on his ascent. I took the crook of his arm, noticing the frock coat's thinning material and fading color, but on Will it was dashing and blended with his black and silver pin-striped trousers. Beneath the coat sleeve, I felt the crispness of his white shirt, probably starched by his doting mother who toiled to make the stand collar precisely pressed, the bow tie precisely knotted.

After a brief, awkward silence, he placed his left hand over mine and glanced at me.

"Your beauty has me tongue-tied, eh."

I reflected back to the day I first met Will, first interviewed at the Sherman, first walked past the opera house and imagined the two of us attending a performance. Coincidence? Fate? No matter, there it was again, an elegant palace, five stories high with the most impressive archway entrance, adorning statues of Painting, Sculpture, Music, and Commerce. Its parallel lined windows reminded me of the uniformity of the Sherman's facade, but that's where the similarities ended. We mixed with a stream of dresses and suits, an increasing hum of locust-like murmurs echoing inside the foyer as we made our way up the grand staircase, past the first floor piano store and confectionery, past the second floor business offices, and then to the rear of the building where the doors opened, a treasure box opened to present a brilliant gem. The auditorium was crowned with a cupola, frescoes painted on its curved ceiling and outlined with golden molding, but the true jewel was above the orchestra, a reproduction of Guido Remi's *Aurora.*

Catherine and I had once read an art magazine with analytical articles about the Baroque period of the 1600s. We were intrigued by the murals that were celebrated, including *Aurora,* but viewing the masterpiece's image in person was heart-stirring with its bold contradiction of colors between night and sunrise. The torch bearing cherub called Morning Star, the soft hued dancers surrounding Apollo (the god of light) being led into the dawn of a new day— magnificent! Will and I could have walked out right then, and our date would have satisfied my dream expectations.

We found our seats on the main floor, and though they were towards the back of the room, any chair would have sufficed. Will took out the program which indicated that the evening would begin with Mr. Theodore Thomas conducting his ensemble in Beethoven's *Overture-Leonora #3*, followed by pieces from Schumann, Liszt, and a new arrangement by Wagner.

"They say this performance is being touted across the country, eh."

"They could play *Farmer in the Dell*, and I'd be happy," I responded with a glow.

The lights dimmed, the musicians stood to take a bow, the audience exploded in applause, and then, as quickly as the clapping emerged, it ceased. Instrumental sounds filled the air, serious in tone and soft in presentation, the strings moved in unison to stir my heart, while the wind instruments chimed in to add an ebb and flow to the rhythm, and when the flutes took center stage, I closed my eyes to feel the bouncing melody, envisioning dancing candle flames. Will touched my knee and pure excitement pulsed through my veins.

As Wagner's *Kaiser March* came to its close, the lights came on for an intermission. I was speechless, breathless.

"Shall we step out for some fresh air?" Will asked.

I simply nodded, still entranced by the lingering song in my head and a reignited desire to stare at *Aurora*. We stepped into the aisle.

"Watch where you're goin', eh," Will blurted as he bumped into my side while I gazed out at the painting.

"What's the matter?" I asked.

"Not sure how that little hoodlum got in here, but didn't he just knock into me." Will pointed off into the throng in front of us, and I caught a glimpse of the boy in question, forage cap and all.

"That's Frederick, who followed me through the market, and he may have been one of the boys with Karl after church. What could he possibly be doing here?"

"Isn't he following again, no doubt. I'm going after him."

"I'm right behind you."

We pushed our way through the mass of people, dirty looks being darted at our backs as we made our way outside. It was nearly dark with just a hint of pink skies in the west.

"There he goes!" Will grabbed my hand, and we ran down Washington Street toward the lake. Three blocks into our chase, panting, the culprit slipped through a passageway and disappeared.

"We lost him," I said, and I could feel sweat beading around my hairline.

Will turned in circles, canvassing the block, but he found no luck in seeing the boy. He turned to me, and his eyes fixated on my forehead. "Liv, you're bleeding."

"What?" I touched my head and looked down at my hand. "It must have been the tree branch that scratched me while running." I didn't know where to wipe my hand. "I hadn't noticed the blood. I thought it was sweat."

Will took out a handkerchief and blotted my face.

"I promise not to sneeze, Will." We both laughed.

"The shop is just down the street a ways. We can get you cleaned up, but we'll miss the rest of the performance."

"I think I've had enough excitement, anyway," I replied. With one hand I held the handkerchief against my head; with the other, I took his elbow again.

The carpentry shop was eerily dark and stagnant, as were the other storefronts down the street. Feeling blindfolded, Will told me to stay put on the stoop while he lit a lantern or two inside. With no difference between eyes open or shut, the other senses heightened— distant train whistles and lapping waves, dried leaves touching on their descent from parched limbs, buzzing cicadas and crickets—an outdoor orchestra finale.

Flickers of light shone through the window, and then Will appeared, a fired wick standing between us, dispersing tiny breaths of heat. We walked into the shadowed space.

"Take a seat there by the tapers, eh, and I'll fetch some water from the pump." He motioned to a work-in-progress upholstered chair which sat next to a bench with three candles lit at varying heights. Before sitting, I lifted a holder and brought the light closer to the tapestry—an elegant lavender fabric, sea-green brocaded leaves and golden vine stitchery.

"Now, aren't ya supposed to be resting *on* the chair, not standing *beside* it."

I continued to stand and admire the work.

"It's Livia-inspired, ya see," pointing to the walnut frame which had an intricate design of carved, swirling Ls, the loops intersecting to form little bows.

"Will, it's extraordinary."

"With a Saturday deadline, don't I have my work cut out for me, eh."

He set the lantern and small water bucket on the bench. "Let me take a look at that cut."

I raised the taper holder to cast a glow on my face.

Will brought his fingers to my forehead and lightly touched the cut. "It's already starting to scab. I'll have to dampen and clean it." His fingers moved gingerly along my temples, his thumbs along my cheek bones. "You're an angel, Livia Haas." His lips inched close to mine and then paused. Without turning away, he took the taper from my grasp and placed it on the shelf at our side. Bringing his hands to my hips, I shivered.

He kissed my forehead. He kissed my nose and cheek. He kissed my lips just once and continued on to kiss my jaw, the tip of my earlobe, the curve of my neck . . . the curve of my neck. It was at the curve of my neck, when I felt his tongue momentarily press on my skin, when hair raised on every part of my body. His lips retreated, and I felt his breath on my shoulder.

"You don't have to stop," I whispered.

I brought my arms up and around his neck, fondled the curls on his head, and guided his face back to mine. My hands took on a mind of their own, sliding down Will's shoulders and chest. They stopped at his waist, aware of the soft leather band around him.

"I want to complete you, Liv," he confided softly.

Jonas' memory, though fleeting, was crystal clear, haunting and reassuring at the same time, *"What do you desire, Livia? Truly desire. I mean, what would complete you?"*

"But we can't. Not now, eh." His words came out in a staggered manner, and he leaned his head against mine.

"I know," I stuttered, propping my head against his chest. "God, forgive me. I'm sorry, Will."

"Oh, my love, don't be sorry." We embraced, and out the corner of my eye, I saw a shadow pass by the window.

CHAPTER 13

Wake me when you get in.

I knew Catherine was anxious to hear details about the opera, but I didn't have the heart to nudge her out of slumber, nor did I know how to explain my desirous thoughts at the carpentry shop. Confusion, in most cases, was easier to resolve when talking it out with my friend, but this time it felt private, between Will and me. I spent the remainder of the night in prayer, seeking grace and attempting to subdue my intimate joy.

Bags of rose petals had been turned to paste, rolled into fragrant spheres, and then pinned to cork and left to dry. Ready for stringing, we had only this evening to prepare the beads for the Feast of the Holy Rosary celebration. Catherine and I were among the volunteers making these special rosaries to distribute to parish children or any other person who didn't have one. I tucked my first completed strand into a pocket for Will.

"Details, please."

"Do you remember the fresco *Aurora* by Reni? We read about it several years ago."

"I remember," she said, while her needle worked its way through the flower pebbles, cherry-red stains already painted on her fingertips.

"I was mesmerized by it, along with every other intricacy in the design of the opera house—the entrance arch, the banister up the staircase, the floors and walls and lighting—"

"Slow down, Liv. I want to hear everything from the beginning. First, how did the dress go over?"

Hard footsteps stomped up the back staircase followed by Franz's banging entry through the door.

"Livia Haas, how dare you! How dare you?" he yelled as he barged in.

Catherine and I both jumped at the same time.

"What is wrong with you, Franz?" Catherine exclaimed.

"What's wrong with *me*? I'll tell you what's wrong. I accused my best friend, my blood brother, of harassing a so-called gentleman, that's what's wrong. I accused him of a violent act in the presence of our little Livia, our innocent little Livia, and you know what I found out, Catherine? I found out that she's nothing more than a whore, that's what I found out!"

I couldn't believe my ears. Catherine must have told him about the Will and Karl altercation. Franz stood tall and strong and unmoving as a tree, punching his fist in the air at me, pointing at me. His rage was frightening. When he called me a whore I gasped at his accusation.

"What on earth are you talking about Franz? How could you believe such a thing?" Catherine called out.

"I got the real story, Catherine. As it turns out, Karl told me what happened on that night. He thought he was protecting her from a stranger's unwanted advances. That's what I would have thought, too, if I saw her pushed up against a building in an alley with her skirt up to her chin and the stranger's hand in places they shouldn't have been!"

"What!" We both cried simultaneously.

"Karl didn't think Livia was easy like that. No, he never dreamed she was a willing participant in such a lewd act! In public no less! So, yes, Karl attacked the stranger who had whiskey on his breath and talked with a slurring brogue, and yes, the mick punched him back and brought poor Karl to his knees and then took off with Liv down the street. He didn't want to embarrass our sweet Livia by bringing it up to me, that's all, and now what do you have to say for yourself, Liv? What!"

"I . . . I . . . I can't believe that you believe *him*," I stammered.

Catherine was between us, and Franz was bright red with hostility. Catherine turned to look at me, and her face was just as deeply colored.

"Catherine, please sit down. You can't get yourself worked up like this," I tried to calm her, but I couldn't keep focus as my eyes flashed back and forth between the couple.

"So you take his word over mine, Franz?" she asked her husband.

"I take Karl's word over Livia's, not yours."

"But Livia's words and my words are one in the same."

"To think that Karl was just about to ask Otto for his blessing in courting you."

"No!" I was horrified at the thought. "I would never—"

"And you've been lying to this whole family," he continued, "by keeping this scoundrel a secret. Don't you see that, Catherine? She's been lying to you, and you didn't know it!"

I caught Catherine as she weaved toward me. I yelled at Franz to get some cool rags. He turned pale and immediately did as I told him. She was dizzy and feeling faint.

"Please help me to bed, Liv," she mumbled.

Franz nudged his way in front of me and took Catherine's hand. "I'll take you, Catherine. You are my wife."

"No," she snapped, pulling her arm away from Franz. "Livia can help me. She is my friend."

Catherine apologized many times for defying our trust by telling my story to Franz, but I understood that she was only trying to do the right thing. I sat with her until she fell asleep. Franz stayed downstairs in the shop, and as I continued my bead work, I heard the sobs of the broken man below me. It was the first time I ever heard either of them raise their voices with one another, and that fact must have been more disturbing to them than it was to me. My eyes weakened through the candlelit night, and soon enough the time came for me to leave the rosaries, tend to the cigars, and be on my way to the Sherman House. Before I left, I checked in on Catherine. I found her and Junior nestled on the floor cot in the bedroom; she had one arm draped across her boy and the other holding her stomach, her baby within. I couldn't imagine sleep until I knew that Will was safe.

CHAPTER 14

Pound. Rhythmic hammers on nails, blowing horns, screaming saws. Pound! Pound! Metallic screeches, shouting voices, wooden knocks and drops. POUND! POUND! POUND!

My fists ached from the pounding, but finally the inside noises ceased and momentary silence allowed my pleas to be heard.

Pound. "Will!" Pound. "Will!"

"Brigid, Patrick, and Columille!" yelled Mr. Magee as he flew open the door. "What on earth is the urgency, Livia? Haven't I almost had a heart attack!"

"Sir, is Will here? I must speak with him immediately."

"Liv?" came the call, and Will appeared with saw dust coating him like a robe.

"I went to your house, but your sister said you were here at the shop." I made the sign of the cross. "You're okay," I said with a calmer tone.

"Of course, now, of course." He wiped his hands on a rag before touching my arm. I coughed from the heavy, dusty air.

Mr. Magee reached out to Will. "Won't you take off that dust coat and save Livia from eating wood scraps for breakfast." The son obeyed, handing the coat to his father who then hung it on a hook near the back door. "Whatever the cause of your frenzy, Liv, we're here to help ya, eh."

"Thank you, sir."

"And don't ya worry 'bout that ruffian. Isn't Charlie here to walk with Will every mornin' and evenin', now." He patted me on the shoulder, and I nodded. "I'm headin' down to the lumber yard to straighten out an order. Your brother and his Margaret will be here in a couple of hours. Keep the doors locked, Will, ya hear me?"

Will gave a slight wave to show that he understood, and when Mr. Magee left, I was sure to immediately bolt the lock.

"What's the panic, Livia? Why were you at my house when you're supposed to be at the Sherman? What's happened?"

I explained what occurred the previous night—Franz's fury, Catherine's collapse and my concern for the baby, the accusations against me and all.

"You're not safe, love. I want to believe that Karl achieved some amusement in telling his stories and now will let things lie. I want to believe that Franz will come to his senses and stand by you and Catherine. I want to believe these things, I do, and if these things really happen, you'd still only be safe if I met Franz and your parents. I need to let them see for themselves that I'm respectable and honest and completely in love with you." He paused and looked at the ground, contemplating. "Livia, as long as Franz keeps up any acquaintance with Karl, that monster will have access to you, and I can not—I *will not* accept that."

"I wish I could say that I feel differently, but that's why I came to find you, Will. I think the same things, and I'm worried about all of us. It won't be hard to keep Karl away this weekend, with the Feast tonight and picnic tomorrow, but I need to introduce you to my parents, Will. The sooner the better."

"Monday. Will Monday work?"

"Yes." I took one of his hands in mine. "More than anything right now, I can't have my parents doubt you before meeting you." My journal was tucked in my pocket, and the newly made rosary beads were wrapped around it. "The first place Mother would look to find details would be here," I said, offering the book to him.

"Your diary?"

"Yes. I don't mind if you read it, Will. It just can't be in my house, and I can't bear to get rid of it. With the exception of my reading, writing has been a great escape for me. Especially when I write about you—about *us*."

"About *us,* eh?" Will loosened the rosary's hug, the beads sifting through his fingers until fully draped and swinging. He flipped through the pages and stopped on the last entry of scrawling ink, the opera house passage. He read it out loud, the first time I heard my words come to life rolling off another person's tongue. Though self-conscious, I found it endearing.

"5 October 1871—*Experiences of a lifetime this evening! But more than anything, I learned something about myself. There's great wonder in the curve of my neck!*"

"You do not have to read the whole passage out loud, Will," I smiled.

His head was still bowed over my pages, but he looked up from the entry. Will had a stare that read my mind, a grin that melted my heart, and his silence spoke more than any words. I stood motionless as he returned to his reading, quietly this time, slowly pacing the room as his eyes moved along the lines. After several minutes, his voice emerged to recite the poem I had written:

> "How bright my world could be, if in your hand
> I place my own! But fear will fiercely pound,
> as quickly as my heart upon the sound
> of words so dear from lips I understand.
>
> Your shimmer leads to grief as fine as sand.
> And if the lights connect across the ground,
> the constellation Truth will then be found.
> I can not stand too close to stars on land.
>
> Without a glow, what then will come of night?
> How can I find my way through streets so dim?
> If not with you beside me as I tread—
> companion to my soul, my eyes for sight—
> there is no sun or moon; the path is grim.
> Our fingers touch; the stars inflame ahead."

He set the diary on the window ledge and walked up behind me. His fingers unbuttoned the back of my high collar until skin was revealed to him. His hands reached around my waist, and I tilted my head to guide his lips to the curve of my bare neck.

"Why do I feel like this is right?" I confessed in a whisper. "As if it wouldn't be a sin, not with you'"

He turned me around to face him.

"Will you marry me, Livia Haas?"

There was no hesitation in my response. "I will."

"I pledge to you and to God to love and honor you, Liv, to

do what's right by you. I do."

"I do," I repeated.

He lifted me into his arms and cradled me against his chest, escorting me this way to the back room and gently setting me on a cushioned chaise. Then he closed the door and came to me.

CHAPTER 15

The fog was lifting from lethargic slumber to groggy consciousness when I overheard their voices from the shop below.

"You're drunk again, Franz."

"It's not the whiskey, Otto. I'm telling you we must hurry. They say it's jumped the river. Don't you hear the sirens?"

I vaguely made out the ringing of bells of which Franz warned, but I was not alarmed. Such was the sound on a regular basis with minor blazes being spurred as a result of the dry conditions.

I sat up on my cot and rubbed my eyes awake, but my sight only adjusted from sleep-darkness to the real pitch black room around me. The hands on the clock appeared to read 1:00 a.m. Or was is 2:00?

"What are you doing?" yelled Father.

"I'm packing the tobacco goods from the counter," Franz replied. "I'll grab the ledger and money box and whatever tools will fit in the sack. Now, go get the women and Junior!"

The urgency in his orders and the tone in which he spoke to Father were uncharacteristic of Franz, but so, too, had been his rant just two nights prior. I rose, stepped quietly past my parents' bed and opened the window.

The fear came not from the muddled sounds of people and horses and carriages in the middle of the night, but rather the acrid smell being tossed upon the wind.

"What is it, Livia?" Mother asked with a yawn.

"It's fire. We must evacuate quickly."

. . . Hail Mary, Full of Grace . . .

Within ten minutes' time, havoc ensued in the streets. No one seemed to know the specific details about the conflagration, but a couple of things were certain: it was not controlled, and it was heading in a northerly direction, directly toward us.

"Put Junior in the wagon," Catherine told Franz as she wobbled out the door.

"We need the wagon for our belongings. He's old enough to walk." Their words were edgy, which told me they hadn't had time to make amends.

Clinging to his mother's layers of frocks and aprons, Junior cried. He didn't want to be pulled anyway; he wanted to be held, but no one could accommodate the wishes of a nine-year-old when hands were already filled with blankets and food bundles, trinkets and tools, and in Mother's case, a large cast-iron pan.

"It's heavy and awkward, Johanna," Father complained. "Leave it behind."

"And it's all I've left from the homeland," and she placed the pan at the bottom of the wagon before Franz could swing the tobacco-filled flour sack on top of it.

Throngs of people were scurrying westward. "Our idea is to make it over the bridge and then pray the flames don't jump again." That was the plan of several neighbors, and we followed.

"Wouldn't it be better to head east to the lake?" I asked. But no one answered, as everyone was preoccupied with their own thoughts and worries.

114

When I noticed a slight weave in Catherine's step, I reached for her elbow to help steady her, and that's when I noticed the dampness.

"Are you okay, Catherine? You're sweating profusely."

She took a deep breath and spoke softly into my ear without slowing her pace. "If I can't keep up, I want you to take Junior and go on."

. . . the Lord is with thee . . .

"Never." I held her tighter, letting her lean on me as the crowd grew denser with each block. Franz, being pushed left and right by the frantic mob, was tugging at the wagon's handle.

"There are too many people," I yelled out to him. "We're not all going to make it across. We'll be trampled to death if the fire doesn't get us first."

His speed reduced and then halted.

"What are you doing, now?" asked Father.

He turned the wheels of the wagon around, right there in the center of a swarm of people. "Livia is right. Before we get even further, let's turn us around and head east, to the water."

"We'll be fish trying to swim against the current! We can't make it through this crowd!"

"We have to try, Otto. I, too, agree with Livia," said Catherine.

Her weak voice beckoned Franz's attention. "Oh my Lord, Catherine," he said, dropping the wagon handle and grabbing a handkerchief from his trousers' pocket. "You are drenched."

"I'm fine." His cloth swiped her forehead and cheeks.

"Everyone, take from the wagon what you can carry, and

we'll leave what we can't hold. I want Catherine off her feet."

"No, Franz. I'm fine." But Franz wasn't listening. He helped her get seated and kissed the top of her head. He took charge, and he plowed us eastward through the sea of bodies pushing against us.

"Be brave, my little man," Franz called out every block or so, and Junior wiped away the tears.

More people joined in the frenzied journey, and from a distance, I made out the human outline forming along Lake Michigan's shore.

Her moan was hardly audible, but it stopped Franz in his tracks. "What is it, Catherine?"

"The baby's coming." Tears streamed from her eyes.

"No. We haven't much further. Hold on Catherine. Please." He looked to Mother. "Johanna, what should we do?"

"Go Franz. As fast as you can," she advised. "You need to get your wife to the lake and find another mother to help deliver this child. I have the shakes, and Livia hasn't the experience."

Catherine started gasping for breaths and reached for Junior. "Be—shhhh—a good—shhhh—boy for your mama—shhhh—shhhh—" She clung to him, and he to her. "I love you, my baby —shhhh—I love you."

> **. . . blessed art thou amongst women, and blessed is the fruit of thy womb, Jesus . .**

The crowd pressed on in earnest, and we let Franz quicken his pace, as Catherine's wagon became engulfed by the horde behind him. Mother placed her Bavarian pan on the ground and took Junior's hand; she then allowed the masses to move them

116

with a group momentum.

"I think I see Dr. Venn," I called out.

"We must stay together, Livia. Do not go."

"But Father, he could help Catherine. Just keep heading towards the lake. Don't go too far north or south, and I'll find you." And I turned in the direction of my sight, praying the doctor wouldn't vanish from my view.

"Doctor Venn!" I yelled as I grappled with the people in my way.

A hand grabbed at my forearm and yanked me up a curb. I tripped, but the clasp of the hand tightened and lifted me against my will to an upright position.

"Let go of me!" I screamed, but the force of his pull kept dragging me through the crowd and led me into a narrow passageway between two homes.

"What's the need for a doctor, Liv?" Karl asked, still tugging at my arm.

"It's Catherine. She's in labor." My chest throbbed. He let go, and when I leaned to get away, he pushed my back against the wall.

"Ah, dear Franz will be a vati again. A good egg, that Franz. I'm lucky to have met him, as was my own vati's plan, I'm sure." His breath reeked, a sour smell of drink. His hands pressed my shoulders into the wooden siding, so hard I could feel a splinter scratching at my spine.

"Please, Karl. I need to reach Dr. Venn." But he didn't hear a single word I said. His eyes looked past me, dreamlike, with pupils getting deeper and larger each second.

"When I saw those papers, his home in Quakertown, his property owned by a Haas, what choice did I have but to dig at him, find my target—Vati's target?"

The smoky, burning odor was increasing, and the heat was building. I tried to wriggle my body away from him, but he wouldn't loosen his hold. "Karl, the fire is getting close. We need to go."

"It didn't take much to cause his delirium, and I asked all the right questions, Vati's questions that were uttered across my tongue. When I learned of Otto, I thought him too responsible and good to be my target. But Jonas—he had the blood, I knew."

Hearing my brother's name being spoken from this monster's lips, made me seethe. Without a second thought, my right hand lifted and slapped Karl's cheek, startling him out of his hypnotic state. I froze too long, stunned by my own action, and he snatched my chin, throwing my head back to the wall. His fingers pinched my jaw firmly, and I couldn't move my mouth.

. . . Holy Mary, Mother of God . . .

"Vati took care of Jonas for me. I needed to get your family here, to find the right Haas for my revenge." He hit my skull against the house again. "It wouldn't have been you, the sweet and pure Livia, until you started hanging with that mick, that rebel. Marrying him would bring children with the blood of a Haas and surely the nature of a radical, now, wouldn't it?" His eyes narrowed. "We can't let that happen, now can we?"

He released my jaw and moved his hand flat on my chest.

"I'm sorry, Karl. Believe me. I don't know what you are

talking about. I don't know what happened to your father, and why you're so consumed with our family, but I need to get help for Catherine. She's not a Haas; she's not a rebel. I beg you to let me go for help before this fire takes us all."

No one could possibly see us in this dark walkway, hidden between two desolate structures, and when I turned my head to look toward the street, I saw the sky lighted above the crowd and buildings, a glow of copper and gold. If I called out to the mobs rushing in the street, no one would hear my pleas above the intensifying shouts of desperation. *Move on! Go faster! It's coming! Get to the water!*

He strummed his fingers along my clavicle, the middle tip tapping inside the recess of my throat.

"Did she believe him?" he asked, his face closing in on mine.

"Who?"

"Did Catherine believe Franz when he told her what I said about that mick, about what he was doing to you?"

"You lied," I said defiantly, though I did not know from where the defiance was coming. My body trembled under his touch, and he could feel it.

"I lied about the mick doing it, but it's what I wanted to do myself." His free hand reached down and started gathering my skirts.

"You can't do this, Karl." My eyes blurred.

"Sorry to disappoint you, little rebel, but I must." Both hands seized my dress. "This is what Vati wants." He pulled the skirt trim into my mouth to gag me. "Your uncle murdered my father." I winced at his mustache scratching my face, slurring the words slowly to ensure that I understood what he was saying. "Your uncle murdered my father," he repeated, "and revenge is going to be sweeter than I thought it'd be, Livia Haas." His body pressed up against me.

. . . Pray for us sinners . . .

Silent screams roared inside me, as I imagined Chicago flames engulfing me. I plunged a hand into my frock pocket; finding my rosary, I clenched until the beads made indentations in my palm.

. . . Now, and at the hour of our death . . .

EVENING JOURNAL – EXTRA

CHICAGO, MONDAY, OCTOBER 9, 1871

Chicago is burning! Up to this hour of writing (10 o'clock p.m.) the best part of the city is already in ashes! An area of between six and seven miles in length and nearly a mile in width, embracing the great business part of the city, has been burned over and now lies a mass of smoldering ruins! All the principal hotels, all the public buildings, all the banks, all the newspaper offices, all the places of amusement, nearly all the great business edifices, nearly all the railroad depots, the water works, the gas works, several churches, and thousands of private residences and stores have been consumed. The proud, noble magnificent Chicago of yesterday, is to-day a mere shadow of what it was; and helpless before the still sweeping flames, the fear is that the entire city will be consumed before we shall see the end.

The entire South Division, from Harrison street north to the river, almost the entire North Division, from the river to Lincoln Park, and several blocks in the West Division are burned.

It is utterly impossible to estimate the losses. They must in the aggregate amount to hundreds of millions of dollars. Amid the confusion and general bewilderment, we can only give a few details.

The fire broke out on the corner of DeKoven and Twelfth streets, at about 9 o'clock on Sunday evening, being caused by a cow kicking over a lamp in a stable in which a woman was milking. An alarm was immediately given, but, owing to the high southwest wind, the building was speedily consumed, and thence the fire spread rapidly. The firemen could not, with all their efforts, get the mastery of the flames. Building after building was fired by the flying cinders, which, landing on the roofs, which were as dry as tinder, owing to the protracted dry weather, instantly took fire. Northwardly and northeastwardly the flames took their course, lapping up house after house, block after block, street after street, all night long.

The scene of ruin and devastation is beyond the power of words to describe. Never, in the history of the world, has such a scene of extended, terrible and complete destruction, by conflagration, been recorded; and never has a more frightful scene of panic, distress and horror been witnessed among a helpless, sorrowing, suffering population.

It is utterly impossible, at the first thought, for the mind to take in any conception of the fearful ravages of the fire-fiend, although the astounding facts stated above, is enough to appall the most heroic. The awful truth of the situation will be more fully comprehended by a glance at the following very imperfect list of the city's loss. It is, however, proper to state that, at this writing, the confusion in the police and fire departments is so complete as to render it impossible to give anything like a detailed account of the terrible conflagration.

PARTIAL DETAILS OF THE LOSSES

The first to be mentioned, and possibly the most startling feature of this carnival of flame, is the total destruction of the City Water Works, by which calamity the firemen are rendered helpless to make the least endeavor to arrest the onward march of the devouring element. Should any other fires occur in parts of the city not burning, they most certainly have their way. At about 12 o'clock last night, the sheet of flames licked across the river to the neighborhood of Jackson street, first igniting a small wooden building, which communicated the fire to the Armory, and soon to the South Side Gas Works, the immense gasometer exploding with a fearful detonation, heard all over the city. Then commenced the fearful ravages, which in a few hours, laid the entire South side in ashes, north of Harrison, the Post Office and Custom House, the Chamber of Commerce, the Court House and the rest soon went down in the ocean of fire and smoke. In brief, the following prominent buildings have perished with, in almost every case, their entire contents: the New Jerusalem Church on Adams street, and the Catholic Church on Desplaines street.

The Journal office, the Tribune, the Times, the Republican, the Post, the Mail, the Staatz Zeitung, the Union, and many other publications.

Crosby's Opera House, McVicker's Theater, Hooley's Opera House, Dearborn Theater, and Wood's Museum.

First, Second, Third, Fourth, Fifth, Union-Northwestern,

Manufacturers' Cook County, and Illinois National Banks.

The Second Presbyterian Church, St. Paul's Universalist Church, Trinity (Episcopal) Church.

The magnificent depot of the Chicago Rock Island and Pacific and Lake Shore and Michigan Southern Railroads, on Van Buren street at the head of LaSalle street. The Great Central Union depot, and the Wells street depot of the Chicago and Northwestern Railroad.

The National Elevator, corner of Adams and the river, Armour, Dole & Co.'s Elevator, corner Market and the river, Hiram Wheeler's Elevator on same corner as the above, the Galena Elevator, corner Rush street bridge and river, and "A" of the Illinois Central near the Illinois Depot at the basin. Tremont House, Sherman House, Briggs House, Metropolitan, Palmer, Adams, Bigelow, European, (Burks), Garden City and the new pacific, in process of erection, on Clark and LaSalle streets.

The following prominent business houses are in ashes: Field, Leiter and Co., J.V. Farwell's block, and all the magnificent blocks in that locality. The Lake Side Publishing company's new building on Clark street, Terrace Row on Michigan Av. and adjacent residences.

Farwell Hall burned at about four o'clock this morning.

The great breweries, on the North Side are gone. In fact, as stated above, the entire South and North sides, from Harrison street northwardly, with a few isolated buildings left standing in some remarkable manner, are in hopeless ruins.

124

HELP COMING

During the night, telegrams were sent to St. Louis, Cleveland, Milwaukee and nearer cities for aid, and at the time of going to press several trains are on the way to the city, bringing free engines and men to assist us in this dire calamity.

BOARD OF TRADE

The Board of Trade has leased for present use the northwest corner of Washington and Canal streets.

We call attention to the card announcing a meeting of the Directors of the Chicago Board of Trade tomorrow morning, at 10 o'clock at 51 and 53 Canal Street.

COUNCIL MEETING – A PROCLAMATION

The Common Council and a number of prominent citizens are holding a meeting this afternoon in the First Congregational Church, to make such arrangements as may be possible for the safety of the city. The Mayor has issued a proclamation that all fires in stoves in the city shall be extinguished.

THE EVENING JOURNAL

We are under great obligations to the Interior Printing Company, 15 and 18 Canal street, for accommodations by which we are enabled to issue this Extra. We hope before many days to be able to announce permanent arrangements for issuing The Evening Journal regularly. We have saved a portion of our subscription books, and hope to be able to resume publication without great delay.

Amen.

*　　　*　　　*

October 9, 1871
Birth Announcement: George Jonas Dietz

*　　　*　　　*

*   *   *

INITIAL LIST OF 175 KNOWN DEAD...
MORE TO COME
FOLLOWED BY OUR UPDATED LIST OF THE MISSING

Known Dead #104
Dietz, Catherine (housewife)

Known Dead #130
Magee, William (carpenter)

*   *   *

CHAPTER 16

December 20, 1871

Dearest Mother and Father,

I have arrived safely at the Sisters of Charity Home. I have a place to lay my head each night and food to nourish my body each day. Though the trip was cold and weary, and this dwelling a place of sorrow, I shall not dare complain, for your conditions are more severe than mine. I miss you, and at times I find myself thinking that this is not me, that these are not my circumstances, that this is all a dream, that I will wake in the morning to the quiet of our flat in the pre-dawn darkness. But sickness greets each sunrise still, emotional more than physical now, as my thoughts return to my memory of you on the day I left Chicago. I am ridden with grief and guilt to be away from you, to be lost in the unknown as to where you are, if you all remain in that single room at Mr. Heinrich's aunt's cottage or if you've had to separate or move on. Dear Lord, what will become of Franz and Junior and that precious miracle, George! I worry that Franz will go mad, that Junior will never smile again, that George will not survive the winter. I worry that you will not receive the financial help that was promised by the Relief and Aid Society. Please keep me abreast of what is happening. I will be thinking of you on Christmas Day, praying to our sweet Jesus and Most Blessed Virgin Mary that better times are coming.

All my love and prayers,

Your daughter,

Livia

"No! No!"

"Miss Haas! Miss Haas!"

"No!"

The shaking of my shoulders and screeching of my name brought me out of the nightmare and back to my surroundings.

"Oh, Sister Anthony!" I clung to the black cape that enveloped me.

"It's all right, child. It's all right."

The episode was becoming more frequent. When I deprived myself of sleep long enough, my body insisted on rest and my mind acquiesced reluctantly. Soon lakefront scenes appeared. *First, I see a snippet of Franz with red-rimmed eye sockets rocking a swaddled bundle back and forth, back and forth mimicking the ebb and flow of tides behind him. Next, a group of men and women, all wearing coats of soot, are huddling around Mother and Father, huddling so tightly I can't make out their faces, but I know their voices, their mumbled voices saying, "She fought for the baby; she held on for the baby; she loved that baby," and each statement follows with the slapping of water as if a refrain to their lament. And then comes the vision of Junior laying atop the blanketed wagon, his head facing down and breathing into the woolen sheet. Catherine's hand is dangling from beneath the trim.*

"It's all right, child. It's all right."

"No!" *I'm tightening my fist around beads.*

"No!" *I'm seeing my tattered frock and smelling the sour scent of drink. Beneath my shoeless feet, I'm feeling the layer of ash that's mixing with sand on the shore. It takes me all night and day to find them.*

"It's all right, child. It's all right."

But it wasn't all right, because then I'd hear the echoes of crashing waves again, and Will would appear beside me—*"I don't condone defiance toward God, ya see..."*

I tilted my head against Sister Anthony's bonnet, and as I sobbed, I let her rock me, back and forth, back and forth. Like the movement along the lakefront.

February 8, 1872

Dearest Mother and Father,

I received your last letter with mixed emotions. Although I'm heartened to hear of baby George's improvements, I am saddened to hear that his future will be fragile with unknown effects from an early and harsh birth. I will continue to pray for his health, as well as yours.

Has there been any hope for jobs? I was encouraged by the thought that workers such as Franz and Father would surely be needed for the rebuilding process, but I was frustrated when reading the advertisements that are being circulated across the country. How can businessmen entice more and more people to come to the city when those already there can't find a place to live? How much homelessness can the city endure? I pray for more sensible leadership, like Police Commissioner Brown. He was the only leader who spoke out against the military presence after the fire. I remember Mr. Brown appreciating the true

*character of hardworking Chicagoans and saying that the militia
faced no chaos to which to bring order on the southwest side, yet
they were stationed there on the demands of businessmen who
feared retaliation for their selfish decisions. Has Sheridan's
soldiers remained on call throughout the winter? Has there been
any violent unrest?*

*I do hope Junior is being a good and helpful boy? Are there
any children with whom he can play? Do you have access to
books for him to read? I pray for that angel every night!*

*As for me, I am growing, I am healthy, and I miss you all. I
miss Catherine, too. I'll never stop mourning for her, like I'll
never stop mourning for Jonas.*

All my love and prayers,
Your daughter,
Livia

Of course, I didn't include the fact that I'll never stop
mourning for Will, either.

Thoughts of Will and Catherine consumed my days and
nights. If it were not for prayer and writing, my mind would
have been that of a lunatic, but my mourning found its outlet in
silent novenas and whispered chants amidst the chaos, in
discarded paper scraps and poetry books amidst the House's
illiterate population. In prayer I pondered whether or not Karl's
attack was punishment for a sinful act with a man I loved, but
remorse was usually replaced with a sense of sorrow. I might
have needed forgiveness, but I couldn't find it in myself to feel

evil and dirty, not when it came to Will. I questioned God's taking of Catherine, why a righteous God could be cruel to a person of pure goodness. In writing I reflected on the depths of my losses with details drawn from that profound place inside one's spirit. Bleak and tormented, I found words for my mute voice, an inside whimper on verge of escape.

They patter, these rain drops, on leaves still green

with summer's breath, recalling dreams of you.

But then, again, the sun and snow do, too.

The nightingale is friend and sets me free

to weather days of clouds and changing hues.

They patter, these rain drops, on leaves still green

with summer's breath, recalling dreams of you.

When morning comes, your image fades. I wean

my thoughts and wash away your voice, renewed.

And then I am reminded by the dew.

They patter, these rain drops, on leaves still green

with summer's breath, recalling dreams of you.

But then, again, the sun and snow do, too.

April 25, 1872

Dearest Mother and Father,

I must admit that my faith is being tested. There is such misery in this place. The Sisters are most giving and patient, and I don't envy their job in having to do what they deem

necessary for separating mother from child, but the whole
process feels so inhumane! Sadness washes over me with the
sights and sounds by which I am surrounded, and my inner
thoughts do not offer any reprieve as I keep imagining what is
happening back home. I pray, but my pleas have yet to be
answered, and then I receive your correspondence, and I am
angered by the lack of care that is being given you. I don't
understand how the mobs of citizens with whom I bumped
shoulders on that horrific night can still be displaced, living in
crowded tents and shanties while mansions are rising up! Your
description of the view, as you walk from the westside cottage in
which you reside to the St. Michael's parish, is exactly as I
remember it when I left. The only assistance that anyone has
received is that of his neighbor who is equally desolate. To
where is the relief money going, this money that is pouring in
from around the world? Has anyone inquired? Or is such a
question not allowed? Oh, I pray! I try to think of the good
things to come, of St. Michael's gutted but still standing and
getting ready for reconstruction, and that is what I want to see as
a sign of hope! But is it enough? I will stop my rant, but oh, the
frustration of not being with you, of being so far away and not
living through this tragedy with you! Be courageous, my dear
parents, and be strong. You have survived the worst, I pray, and
there are Junior and George about whom to think. Franz is
bound to find work soon, and when that happens, he will have a

new sense of purpose and dismiss the alcohol that presently
eases his pain.

Give hugs to the boys for me.
All my love and prayers,
Your daughter,
Livia

Unable to block out my surroundings at the Sisters of
Charity Home, the morbid moans and growing bodies crowded
closer and closer with every month, and I resolved to be a friend
to those around me; it was what Catherine would have done.
Nighttime meant hysteria for lonely-souled women who, without
distraction, got lost in their own thoughts. I became a storyteller,
sharing novel tales in candlelit quarters, reminiscent of days long
gone with Jonas. Some accounts sparked discussions between
my oral vignettes, when the saddest of expectant mothers
confessed their "sins," harrowing details of doomed virtue
which, many times, centered on unwanted advances by male
relatives. My heart ached for these heroines whose life tragedies
were unfolding behind wooden walls of a frame house set apart
from the rest of the world in the center of isolated pastures.

April 17, 1872
Dearest Mother and Father,
What joy to hear that you have received tobacco donations
from our Quakertown friends! It can't be much, but it is surely

something — it's hope! I can't describe the pride I feel with
Junior taking it upon himself to go into the city to sell cigars on
street corners. He is a good boy. I pray that the Heinrichs are
able to secure the apartment of which you wrote. It will be
refreshing to have a place of your own. Our Lord is being
inundated with my prayers for turning tides!

I will not speak of sorrow today. I will concentrate on my
blessings, two of which are you!

All my love and prayers,
Your daughter,
Livia

One night, I woke while the robins uttered their songs, and I
couldn't pinpoint the dream I had had, but it was with me, as if I
had gotten up for only a moment from a lively supper table and
returned to empty chairs, still hearing the echoes of words I
couldn't decipher and feeling a warm sense of encouragement. I
rubbed my protruding stomach and gave my unborn child a hug.
That's when I wrote the letter.

June 20, 1872
Dearest Mother and Father,
I am writing to inform you of a change in plans.
I am not giving up this baby. I cannot do it. Here at the
Home, I've seen the agony of unwed mothers, young and old
alike, who are deprived a single glimpse of their children, unable

to mourn their losses with images of eyes or hair or complexion. What torture it must be! I cannot fathom their deep sorrow, their ever-present regret. What will become of them? Will they see baby ghosts wherever they roam, in the coos of baskets at the park, in the laughter of siblings jumping in the rain, in the tears of lost toddlers at market? How barren their souls must be after delivery, and continue as such for eternity!

I cannot humanly understand the heavenly plan that's been set for me, but I've prayed to our Lord and to the Blessed Virgin. I've asked forgiveness and guidance, and in response I was given a miraculous experience, to bear witness to the birth of my roommate Annie's son and assist in his arrival by cutting the lifeline cord, the last connection between him and his mama. I witnessed his brisk exit, wrapped in cloth blotted with Annie's blood, never touched by the fingers that cried out to hold him. Will he ever know that he was loved by this beautiful woman? Oh, it's impossible to comprehend the empty pit and woeful state these mothers must endure! I shall not be one of them. I shall not!

Shun me if you will, and I will love you still. I will accept your decision as to whether or not I am allowed to return, amid rumors and disdain. I can withstand the mockery, if you can. If you say there is no room, I will understand. Please write back and let me know your wishes, if I should fend for myself and child, or if you will receive us with open arms.

Blessings to you all,

Livia

No matter the baby's conception, whether created in an act of love or violence, I made my decision, and once the reality of motherhood hit me, I was reminded of Hester Prynne and was determined to prepare myself for the worst. No longer the innocent I was just months prior, I needed to be strong, so I folded the letter, placed it in an envelope, and addressed it. I knelt down and said a prayer for God to grace me with a healthy, smoky gray eyed babe.

CHAPTER 17

The humidity hung heavy in the cramped space, but I didn't
complain. No matter the confined dwelling, our temporary
privacy offered more than those in the group ward, where the
dank mold overpowered the sweet smell of breast milk, and the
constant squeals of babes and mothers were indistinguishable,
both desperate for consolation. Walking the five feet to the
basin, there was resistance in the air, and my lungs struggled to
inhale as I tiptoed past her crib, a second- or third-hand bed with
tiny nicks and teeth imprints decorating the loose spindles that
rattled with every movement. At fleeting moments like this,
when her curdling cries and quivering tongue were at rest, when
her drawn eyelids twitched to signal imaginary performances
bouncing in her mind, when a gentle smirk emerged from her
lips as foreshadowing of the mischief she'd cause in years to
come, I was filled with reserved hope.

To my face, cupped hands carried the water, tepid from
basking on the sill in the remnants of the shining sun, and I gave
myself a splash, not so much for cleansing the sweat or
refreshing the skin, as for an excuse to have cheeks dampened by
something besides tears, and I managed a glance in the cracked
mirror. Had my eyes dulled, or had the somber sight of ashen
walls blended into my reflection? I reminded myself that it was
of no consequence. Otelia's eyes were the ones that needed to be
bright, not mine.

"You have a visitor!"

The call startled me, as well as my irritated Tilly.

"Whaaa! Whaaa!"

"Shhh. Shhhh, now, sweetie." All four limbs batted the air; her belly showed short inflations, and her peepers, though closed, bubbled like a brook. My back was to the doorway so that the voice, before vision, came first, just as I reached for her blanket.

"I've come for you, Livia."

Like a statue, he stood motionless in the threshold. His tobacco-colored hair was combed back to straighten the waves, revealing a forehead higher than I had ever noticed, or *had* I ever noticed? Pallid skin and sunken cheeks made his nose appear straighter, narrower, with nostrils so thin I wondered how he could breathe through them, and his serious chin protruded just enough to give a proud air about him, an air I knew to be false. Franz didn't have an arrogant bone in his body. His hands were delicate; however, a kind of hardness came through his blank stare, even when transfixed on the swaddled bundle in my arms.

"Franz." It was the only word that came out, without excitement or resentment, just a statement, as if I were expecting him.

"I was instructed to come, to retrieve you and the baby."

"Retrieve us? You make it sound like we're objects to be repossessed."

The remark was not meant to cut like a dagger, but the honesty of my words must have made him nervous. He took a handkerchief from his trouser pocket and wiped his forehead and then his sweaty palms. Wringing the cloth in his hands, he said with a low and mumbled inflection, "We are to be married."

The announcemnt caught me off guard, and a slight gasp caught my throat.

"Married? You and me?" I rocked Otelia, placing a finger in her mouth to suck and calm her cries.

"Yes," he replied to the floor.

"Is that the condition for me, in order to return home?"

"It is a wish, not a condition."

I placed the settled babe back in the crib and turned toward him. "Franz, we can't. You know that. We don't love one another, not that way."

"Junior misses you. He's had a difficult time of it." Franz cleared his throat. "Your child needs a father, Livia," he said in a rehearsed tone. "My baby George needs a mother. Johanna and I cannot care for his ailments the way we know you could. He took in the fumes during premature delivery, and the results will last a lifetime. He wheezes and can't breathe at times. He is delayed in all the milestones of a new child. We fear for his survival, and this family can't take another passing."

"I can raise the children, Franz, but I can't marry you. I'm sorry, but it's just not right."

"The night of the fire, Catherine was still upset with me. I wasn't listening." He gave a slight cough and wiped his face, still directing his words at our feet. "She told me you loved Will."

The mere sound of his name made my heart drop.

"They are gone, Liv," he continued. "Neither of us will ever wed for love. Ours will be a marriage of convenience for—" He peeked at the bundle in her bed and paused.

"Otelia. Otelia Catherine Haas," I said. "That's the name I gave her."

There was a hint of a smile, but his thoughts seemed far away. "A perfect choice. Otto would have been proud."

His words made me light-headed. "What do you mean, 'Otto *would have been* proud'? What has happened to my father?"

"Johanna wanted to wait until you returned home; she didn't want to write it in letter." Franz glanced at me, briefly. "He's gone too, Liv."

"Gone?" Knees buckling, I sat on the edge of the bed and rang my hands in the baby blanket on my lap. "How?"

"Otto was trying to get his due money from the Relief and Aid Society. We planned on reopening the shop, and we needed our funds. He went with his friend, Mr. Reinhardt, who also needed cash to start over."

"Was he...killed?" I stuttered.

"There was a whole group of them, all round up like cattle and beat down. Otto wasn't strong enough to fight back."

A buzzing sound rang in my ears. *Cicadas. It's appropriate to be aware of the cicadas at the moment I learn of Father's death. "Remember the 17-year cicada cloud back in Pennsylvania?" he had asked when we first heard the clicking and humming in the new city. I remembered.* Tilly's body wiggled about and my hand patted her back out of habit, without emotion or intent.

"We will stop at the courthouse on our way back to Chicago. Your names will change to Dietz." Without waiting for my reply, he stepped into the hallway to fetch an old suitcase. "I will help you pack your things."

It was that simple. The very next day I became Livia Dietz. My husband never looked me in the eye, and the buzzing sound never ceased.

"The probability that we may fail in the struggle ought not to deter us from the support of a cause we believe to be just."

-Abraham Lincoln

CHAPTER 18

George was napping on a mild spring afternoon, and as long as damp cold weather stayed at bay, we had restful hours with the boy, taking advantage of each hour free from worry of pneumonia or ear infections or other ailments that winter months tended to bring. Mother and Tilly were searching the backyard for signs of garden herbs as I took laundry off the line. I hadn't minded the flat that became the home of Mr. and Mrs. Franz Dietz and family. Most of the community was the same as our former neighborhood, everyone sticking together in their rebirth after destruction, and I was welcomed with open arms. George and Tilly were seen as siblings—even though their features had no resemblance—rather than constant companions. I had accepted my roles as wife and mother, as well as daughter, and carried on despite the emptiness that came with so much loss.

"I have wings, Mama!" called Tilly with two pillowcases flapping in the breeze as she ran through the yard.

"Don't get those dirty," I scolded gently. "They are freshly washed and dried, and I need to fold them." After another rotation past the garden, Tilly placed the linens back in the basket and returned to the herbs.

Franz appeared at the back door. He started down the stairs when I asked where he was headed.

"Out," he snapped.

I was accustomed to the bitter responses to my words and actions. Years prior, when the children were toddlers, I had found temporary work in Mother's sewing circle. The wages weren't much, but it was something. Franz, on the other hand, was still unemployed, and with his idleness came resentment and anger. No topic of conversation was safe from his sharp tongue, not even a statement like, "I'm taking Mother and the kids for a walk."

"Where to?"

"If Mother wishes to pay a visit to Mrs. Heinrich, we'll head that way. If not, we'll just walk. The fresh air will do her good."

"Fresh? Ha!"

I had hoped my silence was enough to end the dialogue right there, but he continued.

"With horse crap all over the street?" He took a deep breath. "Ah, now that's what I call fresh. And those screeching streetcars will do the trick for giving you an aching head instead of a clear one."

"We'll be back shortly," I replied, untying my apron.

"Be careful out there."

"We will."

"Wait!" I was about to turn the doorknob, and instead turned toward him.

"What more, Franz?"

"How can you cross a street with only two hands?"

"What on earth are you talking about?"

"Johanna is going blind, and George is deaf. How will you cross them while holding Tilly? Every street is so congested these days. It's dangerous."

I rolled my eyes. "We'll be fine, Franz."

"You don't have to be condescending, Livia. I have a right to be concerned about my family's welfare. Just last week, Mr. Hammersmach's wife and daughter were fatally hit because they crossed the rails a second too late."

"George can sit in the buggy with Tilly. I'll have Mother hold me by the elbow. We'll be all right."

"Fine. Just don't breathe any fumes."

He loathed transportation progress with the clogging of the roads. However, Franz's disgust with this transitional era was briefly altered when his streetcar application was accepted, and he started conductor training on a northside line. We celebrated with pretzels and cinnamon-apples when he returned from his first day on the job. He vowed he wouldn't complain and to only give thanks for having a position. No matter the meager pay, long hours, or hazardous conditions, Franz wanted to see income and stability.

As his life would have it, the tides turned once again for the man. The streetcar workers went on strike. Though he was tempted to cross the strike line and risk the consequences, his conscience wouldn't allow him to do it; Franz understood the importance of the fight. For years the strikers had been promised better pay and an eight-hour day, and it just so happened that he entered the scene when his coworkers had had enough. I respected his decision to join the strike; it was the right thing to do. When he returned from a rally at Market Square, he held his head high, and that sign of self-esteem reminded me of Jonas' pride whenever he spoke of standing up for a just cause. Unfortunately, respect could only carry one so far. Franz lost his income. There were debts to pay, mouths to feed, and George's medical bills were due.

"Can't you use steam and tea again?" Franz asked when I told him I was taking George to the doctor.

"I've tried. It's not working this time."

"How long will this go on? We can't afford to keep taking him to a physician every time he has a cough."

I managed a glare without words.

"I love my son, so don't give me that look as if you care for him more than me," he scolded. "I'm being realistic, not insensitive. I understand his hearing and breathing conditions from birth during the fire. I'm just asking how long it will be before he outgrows these constant infections."

"We don't know." I said.

"The basil and thyme are peeping," Tilly announced.

"Well, that's good to hear. Why don't you help Oma Johanna into the kitchen and wash up. I'll be in shortly."

"I'll take care of this clothesline, Liv," said Junior as he walked through the side gate.

He had grown into a wonderful man, doing all that he could to make life better for everyone around him, so much like his mother in many ways. With Franz in and out of work, Junior never went to school for a long period of time. He would begin his formal education, but then something would come up, and his assistance would be needed at home. I prayed for Catherine's forgiveness whenever this situation occurred. It wasn't in Junior's character to whine, even though he enjoyed his education days. I tried to teach him all the subject matter I knew, and unsurprisingly, he was an avid reader, so he frequented the library as much as possible.

He removed his cap, revealing a halo indentation with the flattening of his thick, mousy-brown hair on top of unkempt curls that draped over his ears and neck. Changes were evident with whiskers making their appearance on a face that had lost all semblance of childhood, a chiseled bone structure with straight nose, full eyebrows, and deep green eyes becoming wiser by the day. He took off his jacket and let his suspenders fall off his widening shoulders, a common routine for the working boy when he got home after hours of selling newspapers on the corner just a mile south of our home, rain or shine, heat or sleet or snow.

"I know the temperatures aren't what we expect this time of year, Junior, but you still need to wear your jacket," I said, picking up the coat and handing it to him.

"I ran most of the way home and got sweated. I'm warm," he replied.

"Even more so, then. I don't want your sweat chilling and making you sick."

"You fret too much," he said as he put his arms though the coat sleeves with a wide grin. "Before I forget, a friend of Father's said to send his regards."

"And who would that be?"

"Do you remember Karl?" he asked, nonchalantly and unknowingly, taking a pair of overalls off the line and meticulously flattening out the wrinkles before making defined creases in the legs.

My face drained of color, a sudden shiver ran from my head to my toes.

"Where did you meet Karl?" I managed to stammer, my voice quivering. I couldn't look at Junior in the eye for fear he'd see my worrisome expression at the sound of that man's name.

"At the corner a couple of hours ago. He's a policeman, and when he came over to buy a *Times*, I placed his change in his hand, but he just stood there staring at me, peculiar like."

"And?"

"Well, I asked him if he needed anything else, and he said, 'No, nothin' else,' and he turned to walk away but stopped and looked back at me. 'What's your name, boy?' he asked. I told him my name was Franz, but everyone called me Junior."

I gave a slight gasp and held Tilly's freshly laundered dress to my face.

"Are you all right?" Junior asked.

"Of course I am," I replied. I took a deep breath. "I'm sorry, Junior. Go on with your story."

He did go on. Junior relayed the conversation between Karl and him. Karl said the boy looked familiar, and after hearing his name he let out a laugh.

"Why, if it isn't little Franz Junior all grown up," Karl said to him.

"I said I vaguely remembered him, and that seemed to agitate him. He said he saved Father during the war and that he was the one who got the family to come to Chicago. Is that true, Liv?" I nodded with a forced grin. "He seemed to know all about Johanna and Otto, too. When I told him that Otto died, he kind of snickered, which I found an odd reaction. He said, 'Stubborn but kind – that's what I recall about old Otto. Nothing like his brother who couldn't keep his yap shut and stay outta trouble. Yes, siree, poor Otto. May he rest in peace.' And he smiled all the while, as if he liked your father well enough but was happy he was dead."

I couldn't speak. Paranoia set in, as if Karl was around the corner, or in the alleyway, or maybe down the street. I wanted Junior to tell me everything, but I didn't want to alarm him with my internal worries, so I concentrated on my laundry task as he spoke.

"He asked about you, too."

I dropped the basket of clean clothes to the ground. That was the last thing I remembered before waking on our couch and seeing Franz leaning over me, holding a cool cloth against my forehead.

"You hear me, Liv? You see me?" he was asking.

I blinked.

"Thank God. You had me a nervous wreck." He wiped my face, gave me a sip of water, and then sat down in the chair beside me.

"Did Junior tell you who he met today?" I asked, still foggy.

"He did."

"Did you ever tell Karl that I had an Uncle George?"

"What do you mean?" Franz responded, puzzled.

I repeated my question.

"I don't know. I could have. What does your uncle have to do with Karl?"

Your uncle murdered my father. The words came flooding forward, crashing their way into my thoughts. *Revenge is going to be sweeter than I thought it'd be, Livia Haas.*

"How much do you know about Karl, truly know about him?"

"I haven't much memory of our war days."

"And after the war? What did he tell you about himself after our arrival in Chicago?"

"Not enough, I guess."

"You guess? You had us traipsing into this city under Karl's direction, you were indebted to the man more than your own family, and you can't tell me anything? Anything at all?"

"And what is that supposed to mean, Livia? Do you think I'm holding information from you? Do you think my lack of "Karl" discussion has something to do with secrets?"

I didn't respond.

"My God, Liv. You think I knew that Karl's vengeance was directed at your family? That I was an accomplice to his madness? That I knowingly jeopardized your lives?"

I raised my voice. "Maybe there's more to Karl about which we should have known. All we knew was that he was in the army with you, he conned you into moving here, he freeloaded and destroyed the lives of both of our loves, and . . .and . . ."

"Don't, Livia. Don't go back there," Franz demanded.

"Don't go back there? Back there?" I exclaimed. "Back there is in here, Franz," I yelled, pounding at my heart, "and in here," I yelled louder, holding my head.

"I know, Liv, but there's nothing—"

"Nothing!" I interrupted. "Right, Franz. There was nothing we could do back then, when that monster spit on me in the rubble and dust!"

"Liv—"

"And there was nothing we could do when he raped me in the ashes and tore me apart, body and soul!"

Franz buried his head in his hands.

"Nothing, Franz! Nothing is what I became, inside and out! For ten years I've had to deal with nothing! Is that right, Franz?"

"No! NO!" he cried out. "I know you've had to deal with this. I was there when you told your parents. I was there! But I had just buried Catherine. I was holding a sick newborn in my arms and throwing dirt on my wife's grave, for God's sake!" He started pulling at his hair, as if trying to pluck out the remembrance. "What, Liv? What was I supposed to do? You don't think I wanted to kill him? Is that what you want from me now? You want me to get a pistol and murder a cop? Say the word, Liv, just say the word, and I'll do it! I'll sell my soul to the devil and strike the filthy bastard down if it will erase that memory and take away your pain, if it will bring back Catherine, bring back Will! If taking revenge on Karl will set things straight, I'll burn in hell, but I'll do it! I'll do it!"

Franz kept screaming "I'll do it!" My head ached.

"STOP!"

CHAPTER 19

"Please, sir, please! We just need a small payment. Just enough to feed my starving family. I'm not meaning no harm!"

Mr. Reinhardt was grabbed by the sleeve and pushed into the crowd.

"It's a disgrace, I tell you! Herding us like cattle! Where you leadin' us, sir? Where?"

The Relief and Aid Society building, where the march began, was disappearing behind the throngs of desperate citizens being pushed down the street.

"Sure, the Kleins got assistance to regain their fortunes, but there ain't a dime to spare for those who lost their livelihoods! Where's the justice in that, sir? Where!"

Mr. Reinhardt wouldn't let up. The hollering got louder and louder as the masses moved on, away from the Society and closer to the tunnel which ran beneath the Chicago River. The stench grew, the light dimmed, and everyone started to tremble.

"I'm leaving! Can't you see that? I'm leaving now, so let me out of here!" But no one was leaving, and the claustrophobia intensified as every marcher was pressed forward until they met a human wall. Father appeared from behind Mr. Reinhardt's stocky frame. With no place to turn, the clubs came beating down on heads and backs, a message to never demonstrate again.

"I'm leaving! I'm leaving!"

"Livia!" Mother called out. "Livia, wake up!"

My hands were covering my face. I could no longer see the images of my dream, but the memories lived on, resurfacing when my guard was down.

"What were you thinking about this time, Liv? From where were you leaving?"

"Nowhere. I'm not going anywhere."

But that wasn't completely true; if not my body, my mind went places without my consent, and there was a forever fear of heavy clubs, fear of smoky scents, fear of a German soldier's grunts and laughter.

CHAPTER 20

"Moving in today?" she asked.

She was a colored woman, lighter in complexion than my dear friend, Clementine, for whom I prayed every day. Her black hair was held up with dainty clips at the back of her neck and laid in loose curls and waves like a well-kept nest atop her head. She had perfect lips and nose, and a touch of color was applied to her mysterious, deep eyes. I hardly noticed the pause I took on the stairwell on my way to the second floor flat to which I was lugging the family clothes.

"Yes," I replied, setting down the awkward trunk. "I'm Livia Dietz."

"It's a pleasure, Livia. My name is Lucy." She held out her hand in introduction. A cry wailed from her apartment. "My Albert Jr.," she said. And then she smiled and retreated.

The brief meeting struck me. Maybe it was because of her skin, that skin so many Americans hated and degraded, the skin of a people that had once divided our country and was still setting off riots for no other reason than her smooth chestnut surface.

"Keep movin', Liv," bellowed Franz in the entranceway. "This box of kitchen wares is no light feather, you know,".

"Did you remember the box of books, too?" I asked, picking up the trunk again.

Junior was already on the second landing and called down the wooden staircase. "The books were the first items packed and the first items *un*packed."

He pranced along the steps with an energy I could not fathom and relieved me of the clothing burden.

Within days of Karl's appearance, we moved into the tenement located on Mohawk, just four blocks northwest of St. Michael's. It felt necessary to relocate to get a sense of security, to get away from Wells and Division streets, the intersection shared with Karl when he asked Junior where we were living. The new brownstone was designed with flames in mind, as were all of the fresh construction blueprints in areas where owners could afford to purchase bricks instead of wooden materials— another security feature that eased my mind. Even the sidewalks in this part of town were paved, replacing the planks that scattered the pre-fire streets. The building's façade was plain, a rectangular canvas with simply lined parallel windows, three in a row for each of the two flats, and buff cement steps. The identical façade, windows, and stoops could be seen all the way down the avenue, where only the landlords or tenants diversified the block with personalized touches, such as small flags or flower beds or a bit of colored paint around the trim. At 1908 Mohawk, we had a metal slab above the front door that read - 1908 Mohawk. The owner didn't fuss about the property, so he told us when we signed our rental agreement that we could do whatever we wanted in the backyard, as long as we were neat about it and didn't make any trouble with the other tenants and neighbors; however, the front was off-limits because he didn't want to change things up for one renter, when the next renter might want something different.

Our flat was roomy for a "double," but not after six people

settled in. The advertisement stated it was "fully furnished" which meant one bed and one dresser in each of the two bedrooms, a couch and end table in the living room, a small desk and chair in the parlor, a three-shelf pantry with icebox and wood stove in the kitchen, and that was it. No table or chairs for a family to share a meal, no curtains or rug.

"I guess I was right to have saved those second-hand stools. I couldn't part with them because they reminded me of Father, the way he straddled the seat all bent over the tobacco leaves or over the "books" or counter getting a bite to eat. He always preferred the stool to the chair because he claimed that the arms and back were too restraining."

"I'm leaving to pick up Johanna and the kids from Mrs. Heinrich's place, so I'll stop by the old apartment and get the stools. They're still in the shed out back, right?" asked Junior.

"I believe so," I told him. "Have your father go, too. You'll never fit them all in one wagon, but Franz can take the wheel barrow, too, and there's no sense in making you take two trips."

Junior walked over to me and gave me a hug. "Things will turn out all right, you know," he assured me.

"You're a fine young man, Franz Junior," I whispered. "Your mother would be proud."

Junior gave a sheepish grin and grabbed his cap. Franz was out the door moments later, and peeking out the front window, I watched father and son stroll along the tree-lined street. Though still young saplings for the most part—being planted just six years prior— I could see great potential in its scenic charm. Junior was right to be optimistic; life was going to be all right.

As if the angels were agreeing with my thoughts, I heard the mighty bells of St. Michael's ringing in the distance.

Returning from the market later that week, I met Lucy in the stairwell again.

"So you truly don't mind?" she asked.

"Lucy, using the storage room for a dressmaking shop is a marvelous idea, and I don't mind one bit that you're starting a business down there," I assured her.

"And your husband would agree?"

"Why wouldn't he? We're not using it anyway, and who knows, you just might be a big hit and need an extra seamstress to assist you." I smiled at her. "And I would accept such a job on the spot."

"I didn't know you were a seamstress, Livia. Where do you work?"

"When my mother's sight began to fail her, I replaced her in a local sewing circle, but now I'm at the fabric factory down on Lake Street."

"I've heard awful things about that place."

"The hours are harsh," I agreed. "Personally, I'd rather be in the circle still, where I could at least get up and stretch instead of the hours upon hours of being hunched over that machine, but the lighting is just as bad. The only reason I switched is because I bring home about fifty cents more each week."

"Is this lighting the cause for your mother's blindness?" Lucy questioned.

"I'm afraid it is," I told her.

Lucy's eyes narrowed and her mouth curved down into a frown. "Livia, you do realize that I'm blacklisted at the factory, and that my husband Albert and I are quite active in the labor movement, right?"

"I've heard as much, but honestly, Lucy, I don't have time to be up on politics these days."

"I understand time restraints, but you should at least come hear what we have to say about unions and the eight-hour day plans. We're having a rally at Exposition Hall."

"I'll think about it," I said.

"Please do, Livia, and thanks for being supportive about my taking over the storage room." She turned to walk toward the basement, but I touched her arm, and she stopped.

"I'm the one who should be thanking you, Lucy. It's people like you who I admire most in this world. People who stand up and make sacrifices for a cause, people who give voice to those who can't speak for themselves, for whatever their personal circumstances."

"Changes are on the horizon, Livia, mark my words. It may not be tomorrow or next week or next month, but changes are coming." She waved her hand over her shoulder and continued down the staircase.

Changes. Everyone was certainly due for some of that, and if anyone would be at the forefront of such changes, Lucy and Albert were sure to be the ones. As an interracial couple, they were not afraid of raising a few eyebrows or ruffling a few feathers.

Our sewing section faced east, so the morning hours were the least straining on our eyes with plenty of sunlight. For those who had had some rest and a bit of breakfast, the 7:00 a.m. to noon shift was also the most productive with more precise concentration and fewer episodes of body aches and stiffness. Apparently, I wasn't the only seamstress who got word of the rally, as whispers tiptoed above the humming sounds of our machines. Whether or not my coworkers planned on attending the meeting couldn't be grasped by the incomprehensible bits and pieces I overheard. Being seen and identified at the gathering could be dangerous. If such an event occurred, the lightest punishment would be a fine, and when so many employees had to purchase their own threads and needles, or for those who worked part-time from home using their own candles and material and supplies, I couldn't imagine many women risking a cut in wages that were already minimal to begin with.

At noon, there was a rush to eat and use the outhouse, and it was then that the murmurs became coherent. The basic consensus of the talk from the English and German speakers was one of hope, but not necessarily action. Few seemed to be willing to go to Exposition Hall, but one of the older workers told a group of us that she had recently had the chance to listen to Albert Parsons speak, and every one of us should make a point of doing the same.

"Someday we'll have justice and equality, girls. We will be rewarded for our toil and treated fairly in the workplace, and never, NEVER will my daughters and granddaughters have to endure the work conditions we face today," she encouraged us.

"Think about it, now, won't you. Our checks reflect work for an eight-hour day, yet we're clocked in for 12-16 hours without compensation. We must fight for fairness in the workplace, fight for ourselves as well as the unemployed who deserve our second shifts and checks of their own."

"Are you going to the rally, then?" asked Sarah, the young seamstress standing next to me who couldn't have been more than fifteen.

"I am," the elder replied.

"I'll pray for you," Sarah said, and the woman patted Sarah's shoulder.

Franz was insistent about my absence from the rally.

"I went with the streetcar workers, Liv. I felt empowered and filled with hope, but everything was for naught. I can't afford losing another job, and now that I have a position in the cigar factory, we can't take any risks."

The disappointment was shown in the dip of my head, the fidget of my fingers as I unfolded a fresh apron from the laundry basket.

"Not now, Liv. Now is not our time to get involved."

How many others felt the same way? How many others had to put up with fear and succumb to scare tactics?

"Very well, Franz," I replied, tying the smock around my waist. "Dinner will be ready within the hour."

I reluctantly submitted to Franz's wishes. I understood that we couldn't jeopardize our employment, and even if we recruited thousands of workers to come to the rally and risk their jobs, there'd be thousands more desperate souls ready and willing to take our places. *Whose places did we take over ourselves at the factories? What were the circumstances for those we replaced?* I wasn't Uncle George or Will or Jonas; they would have surely attended. I wondered what Catherine would advise me to do.

Long before the sun came up, I sat sleepless at the kitchen table gazing into my tea cup, the flickering flame of a taper sitting center on the table. Inside, my nerves couldn't release the undeniable feeling that Franz might be mistaken, that now was the time, indeed. Contemplating my days at the Sherman, I thought it foolish to have appreciated the splendor of handsome men in their shined shoes, ties and tails and perfectly pressed shirts that dazzled with diamond cufflinks, proper human dolls clinging to their arms with bejeweled hands and painted faces, dressed in silk blouses and skirts of satin and lace, matching hats and parasols to boot. Father understood more than I acknowledged back then. His world was controlled and manipulated by the very patrons on whom I doted, and although the income was welcomed, my employment at the Sherman had to kill him inside.

In the stillness of the hour, I felt a pressure on the back of my hand, as if it was being held. *Both Uncle George and Father rubbed elbows with the 48ers, but our father stopped all that when we were born. He didn't want to take risks when kids were at stake.* For a moment, Jonas' words brought insight into our father, his decisions, his hostility. For my family, I, too, needed to acquiesce to the demands of an employer who became more

163

cruel and unjust with each passing week; it was the reason Father fought to hang on to the farm and then the shop, so as to never have to bow to another boss again.

Outside a dog barked, and the sound snapped my attention back to the tea cup by then cooled, and the candle wax cascading over the plate of its holder. I would be late if I didn't get moving, and I knew that that was all it took to be fired promptly, so I blew out the dwindling flame.

CHAPTER 21

He raised his head and hands to the Lord, his protruding gut masked behind the smooth marble pulpit.

"Does He not understand your anguish? Did He not sweat and toil the same as you? Who amongst you can claim to have a harder life? More pain? More strife?" His face scrunched into folds like the creases in his cassock's flapping, white sleeves. He continued, "In your suffering, you will find God's favor; in humility, His reward. But complaint and greed, my friends? Be warned about those sins, for complaint and greed will be received with His holy wrath!"

Silent tension hung from the rafters, filling space between every stained glass window and hovering about the shoulders of the congregation.

"This is why I shouldn't have gone," Franz muttered vehemently. "Who does the monsignor think he is? What kind of message was that, to be gracious and merciful to our bosses? To see poverty as a blessing in the eyes of God?" His arms flailed for emphasis.

After years of moving from job to job, sometimes going months with none at all, Franz, with good right, had become a cynic, and his current employer at the cigar factory was increasing hours without increasing pay. Junior pulled his brown flat cap to just above the eyebrows and slowed his pace, so his father could take a solo lead on the walkway. "Let me take the wagon," he whispered, releasing the rusty handle from my sweaty grasp. George took no notice of his conductor's change, and Mother quietly took my hand as we solemnly strolled. Tilly was oblivious to the tone as she skipped alongside the wagon.

Franz's open and dramatic rants wore on me, and when his tirade lulled, I spoke with a monotone and calm inflection. "Instead of complaining, we could always join the cause and take action."

Franz whipped his head around. "What did you say?" he demanded.

"I'm just saying that all you do is gripe and cuss. And you direct those comments at me or the kids or my mother. We are not to blame for your disappointments, Franz; we have our own, too. If you want to keep complaining about life's miseries, then isn't it time we complain to the right people and do something to change it?"

He glared at me, despising any moment when I tried correcting him in public.

"I'll be home later." The words fumed from behind clenched teeth, and then he turned the corner and walked into the nearest saloon.

"If he comes home drunk again, there might be a stormy night ahead of us," said Junior.

"There's no 'might' about it," Mother interjected. "You set my rosary by my seat, Livia. I will start a novena tonight." She held on to me a bit tighter, and we continued down Mohawk until we reached our building. Lucy and her friend Lizzie were sitting on the front stoop, and I noticed Lucy looking pale.

"Junior, I'd appreciate your getting Mother and the kids

166

settled. I'd like to greet our neighbor, and then I'll meet you all inside."

Lizzie spoke first. "Ah, the bells of St. Michael's are singing their weekly proclamation, I see."

"Pardon?" I asked.

"The proclamation, Liv. The time of transformation when innocuous worship ends and wallowing consumption begins."

Lucy nudged her companion and straightened her posture. Her hands pressed against her lower back while taking in a breath.

"Don't mind Lizzie's words of religious resentment," she said on exhale. "Sometimes an atheist feels the need to preach, too."

"Atheist?"

I was grateful Mother was not present to hear that word. Surely she would have let go my elbow in order to make the sign of the cross, maybe grabbing at her heart or starting a rosary right then and there, even without her beads. Lucy's eyes looked heavy.

"Are you feeling well?" I asked.

"She's fine. She just needed some fresh air after being cooped up in that storage room," Lizzie answered.

"It's a dress shop, Liz, not just a storage room." Lucy looked up at me. "I'm four months along, and although the nausea has ceased, I still feel lightheaded."

"Well, congratulations to you and Albert," I said. "I didn't know."

"I guess we don't see much of each other for you to notice my thick ankles and swollen hands. I feel my face filling out, too." She patted her cheeks.

"You're stunning, Lucy, and as a matter of fact, now that you mention it, I do see a glow in you."

"I said the same thing," Lizzie chimed in.

"Stop," said Lucy, and she stood to give a stretch. "You'd think that with us living in the same building we'd know each other better, Livia. I didn't know you were religious. Catholic?"

"Yes."

"Devout?"

"I try to be, but sometimes it's hard. There are times I come out of church with spiritual truths and real life answers, and then there are times when I leave with only questions. Unfortunately, today was the latter." I took a deep sigh.

"I have faith, too, Liv. It's just that my faith is in people, not gods."

Lizzie added, "And not people who *act* as if they're gods."

"From where I'm coming," Lucy continued, "I understand that many good people happen to be religious, it's true, but on the other hand, too many of the religious are not necessarily good people. Clergymen take money and bribes all the time from elitist Protestants and Catholics and Jews."

I thought of the monsignor's comments. *Was he bribed by factory owners to make those remarks to prevent anymore of the congregation from getting involved with the laborers' movement or becoming sympathizers?* I pondered Lucy and Lizzie's statements. *My faith is in people, not gods.* I understood what the ladies were saying, but I was reluctant to agree with the idea of atheism. "Like I said," I told them, "today's sermon left me with many questions, so this might not be the best time to debate the importance of religion. I will, however, gladly participate in such a discussion on a different day." I grinned. "In the meantime, Mrs. Parsons, I will be praying for you and that little angel inside you, whether you believe in prayer or not."

"That's the great thing about being a non-believer while having friends of all faiths, Mrs. Dietz. If there isn't a God, then good for me for not having wasted my time with religion. But if there is a God, so many prayers are being offered up in my name, maybe God will be merciful."

Lizzie's lack of piety and Lucy's lackadaisical attitude toward prayer triggered a protective response to my faith, a response that surprised me because of the questions that had recently infiltrated my thoughts. "The way I see it, Lucy, if there is no God, then all I've done is use time, not waste it, in trying to exemplify goodness. However, if there *is* a God, then my soul is further ahead of yours on the stairway to heaven, and I'll have no need for mercy."

From the back entrance, I heard George's pounding fists and verbal grunts, but Tilly's laughter eased my concern and hinted that all was well. I passed through the kitchen with tableware still awaiting my attention from breakfast when the family hurried out the door for Mass. The children's noises turned to joyful squeals as I walked on through the narrow hallway, stopping to peek in on the bedrooms to my right to see which occupants tidied up in the morning before coming out to table. The pounding and laughter swelled, and I smiled, finding Junior with *The Old Farmers Almanac* in his hands, insisting he would read the stories out loud.

"Ha ha! You are silly, Junior!" Tilly cried. "That's not what George wants, and you know it!"

George covered his mouth with one palm each time Junior held up the book and asked, "Is this what you want?" The boy's head flung from side to side to signal his negative response; spiral locks extended in each direction for dramatic effect, and Otelia howled, "No Junior, not the Almanac! He wants Jill and Jack! Ha ha!" She foisted the Louisa May Alcott book into his face.

"Oh, now I see! *Jack and Jill* is what George wants, but Tilly called it Jill and Jack, and I heard it as the Almanac—"

At that, George and Tilly clapped vigorously, and I, too, participated in the celebratory applause. I sat on the floor next to George's chair, and I felt his fingers twirling my hair. I looked up at this miracle of life and love, and I kissed his fragile fingertips one at a time. I patted my legs as a gesture to ask if he'd like to sit on my lap, and George beamed with approval. The day would soon come when he and Tilly would outgrow such an act, but for this day, I relished that time spent with my boy leaning back against my chest, my girl nestled at my side, and Junior reading from *Jack and Jill* until the oral adventures tired out the children. While they napped, I tended to the house chores, even though I desired nothing more than to join George and Tilly in their peaceful rest. Rest. Sometimes it would come, and sometimes it would not.

The lake splashed in the near distance, ice blue with white tipped peaks upon the waves. The gentle crashing and then calming recession soothed me and offered a moment of serenity. His arms hugged me. I was at peace, until I heard him speak in a repeated whisper, "I don't condone defiance toward God, ya see, but won't I forever encourage the questioning of mere men . . . won't I forever encourage the questioning of mere men . . . "

I woke with a start. Franz snored, reeking of whiskey. I heard the quiet breathing of Tilly and wheezing of George, the rattling of branches outside the half open window, and the voices of drunkards somewhere down the alley. I was returned to reality, away from the beach memory of my dreams, yet Will was still whispering in my ear, "...won't I forever encourage the questioning of mere men."

CHAPTER 22

Twilight shadows draped the open lot. By the time I arrived, the dwindling crowd of protesters lingered in pockets around a makeshift stage. Simple choruses, muffled by the traffic and distant trains, continued their response to the last speaker. "Eight hours for work! Eight hours for sleep! Eight hours for what we will!"

The meeting had been brief, and though I had no intention of sharing a voice, I felt compelled to go, to listen to *the questioning of mere men.* "We will meet next week at the *Alarm*," said Albert Parsons as he stepped down from the soapbox, and a mumbled sound of agreement murmured from the men who reached out to shake each others' hands. Albert walked directly to his wife and helped her stand from a bench. She caught my eye.

"Livia?" Lucy gave my elbow a light squeeze. "I'm glad to see you."

"I just wanted to get a glimpse."

"Well, no matter how short or long you've been here, I hope you're impressed with whatever you heard and saw."

"Mrs. Parsons! Mrs. Parsons!" My neighbor was summoned by a group of women across the street. She turned to them and put up her hand to say "one moment."

"Will I see you again?" she asked.

"Of course," I replied.

"I don't mean around the neighborhood, Liv. I mean, will I see you at another gathering?"

"I hope so, Lucy." She smiled and turned away.

Eight hours for work; eight hours for sleep; eight hours for what we will. The chant was replaying in my mind, and I found myself strolling to the beat of the words.

"Liv?" The tap on my shoulder came as a surprise.

"Sarah?"

"My cousin was injured on the job last week, and she's been let go for ineptitude." She paused. "It's unfair, Liv. No one showed her what to do, but she was expected to work a machine anyway."

Her story was typical, but I had no words of consolation.

"I have to get home," she said before I could summon a response, "but can we talk soon?"

"Yes, Sarah. We will talk soon."

"God bless you, Liv." The young seamstress gave me a hug and whisked herself down the street. My eyes followed her hurried retreat, admiring Sarah's innocence and kindness, and then my heart dropped.

No.

It was difficult to get a clear look at the faces beneath her veil and the brim of his hat, but I saw the joined silhouette as Sarah raced by them. His hand touched the button line of onyx teardrop dots against a flat satin canvas leading up to a small standup collar and down to a full back skirt; a drooping bow hung like her deflated shoulders. *Who was she, this widow who accepted the touch without flinching, as if it was expected? Why did he naturally place his hand on the small of her back, as if it was his right to brush his fingers against her, this widow? Is it him?* It couldn't be. *But his hands!* I recognized those hands, no matter how much time had passed. I dreamed about them every night, the rough and gentle intermingling of calloused fingertips and smooth palms that touched my features in the candlelight.

They continued down the walkway before I could catch my breath, before I could speak and call out to him. And as the couple drifted around the corner, the man's cleft chin lifted and turned in my direction. *Will!*

CHAPTER 23

For weeks I couldn't rid myself of Will's image. My mind played tricks on me at the marketplace, and I tracked men of similar height and build until their faces revealed my foolish pursuits. I found myself crossing streets to get a closer look at the hands of those reading at the newsstand. Passing demonstrations became an obsession, and once, when a gathering came to a close, I stood vigil at the streetcar stop, anticipating a reunion with Will's reincarnated ghost.

Stop it, Livia, I reprimanded over and over again, the realistic side of my brain putting the emotional side in check. *I know what the obituary said, but I also know what I saw!*

Needing to bring an end to this distraction in daily life, I decided to find Lucy, to ask if she knew of the mysterious couple. I never seemed to get an opportunity to see my neighbor at the tenement, so I had a better chance visiting her at the office where she and Albert practically lived while switching gears from the all German publication *Arbeiter-Zeitung* to editing and writing the English paper *The Alarm.*

It was located on Wells; the exterior wouldn't catch the attention of a passerby if it weren't for a storefront sign and flyers posted on the windows and glass door. I was hesitant to enter, but just when I was ready to retreat, I thought I caught a glimpse of Will heading in my direction. It wasn't him, of course, but my pause gave the stranger time enough to approach and offer to open the door for me.

"After you, ma'am."

Round drawer pulls lined the wall of cabinets, with wooden pigeonhole storage and counter space filled to the brim; strewn papers cluttered the flat surfaces, while crumpled papers overflowed the metal baskets beside every mismatched chair and ink stained desktop. Though deep, the narrow room was an example of organized chaos, as obvious stations were in full motion with task masters rattling off a litany of directions for each eager volunteer.

"Can I help you?" asked a slight woman, wrinkles adorning a welcoming smile.

"I'm looking for Lucy Parsons," I replied, my gaze still wandering to and fro.

"She might have already left, but I'll check in the back. May I ask who's calling?"

"Livia Dietz."

She nodded and excused herself. My eyes followed her as she wound her way through the maze of workers. When she opened the door to the rear room, steady hums and rhythmic clicks from unseen machines created a background beat for the spirited talk, and together, the sounds played like an orchestra. From the planked floors to the high beamed ceiling, there was a purposeful energy that bounced through the air. The woman disappeared into the commotion, and within moments Lucy emerged from the depths and spied me standing at the entrance.

"What a surprise to see you, Livia."

"I apologize for disturbing you, Lucy. I had no idea of the activity and responsibility that goes on here."

"Around the clock it seems some days, but our work is for

the good of the working class, and the dedication of everyone you see will pay off in due time."

"Well, I won't keep you. I just have a simple question, and then I'll be on my way."

"Is something the matter?"

"No, no," I reassured her with a touch of her arm. "It's about a couple I saw at one of the demonstrations." I inhaled and then exhaled the embarrassment of my request. There was no turning back. "The woman was a widow, dressed all in black and wearing a veil, while the gentleman wore black, too. He would have been about 5'10" with brown hair, smoky gray eyes, and a cleft chin. He would have had an Irish brogue."

"I can't say that I remember meeting such a couple," she answered. "I'm sorry."

I must have placed my fingers on my own chin while describing Will, and when Lucy told me that she did not recognize the couple, I moved them up to my mouth, catching my breath.

"Are they friends of yours?" she asked.

"I was hoping so."

"If you wish, I could inquire with the other speakers."

"Oh, that's not necessary, Lucy; it was just curiosity more than anything else, and I do apologize for barging in like this for such a silly question."

"No problem at all, Livia, but I should return to my writing."

"Of course." I didn't move.

"Is there something else I can help you with?"

"Are all of these people volunteers or are they employed?"

"Almost everyone is offering up their time, but since many don't have jobs, they don't mind sparing a few hours at the office."

"Hmm."

"Interested in joining us?"

"Tilly! I could use some help with supper!"

Otelia had locked herself in the bedroom ever since she got home from school, and having to call out to her three times was uncharacteristic of a typical response. Pouting, she plopped down at the table.

"What subject has you so caught up?"

"The subject of stupidity," she huffed.

I dried my hands, set the carrots and knife to the side, and sat down across from her. "Talk to me," I said.

"They're picking on George again, Mama, and I know I'm supposed to ignore them, but I can't."

My heart sank and head bowed above prayerful hands.

"What did they do this time?"

"There's a group of boys that limp around and make horrible noises. They do it at recess when the teacher isn't looking just to get a rise out of me."

"Darling, I know their actions hurt, and it's not fair that they do these things, but reacting will only give them satisfaction. They probably have their own struggles to deal with, and the only way they feel better about themselves is to pick on other people. If not George, they'll poke fun of someone else, right?"

"Well, I wouldn't know because George is the only mark they have when they're around me."

"Is George a happy child?" I asked.

"Yes."

"Then, it doesn't matter what others do because he is content with who he is, and he teaches us every day to accept our hardships and appreciate our blessings."

"Well, my hardship is having to deal with 12-year-old blatherskites who—"

"Who probably need to be educated more than anything else."

"How am I supposed to educate them, Mama? I'm just a girl."

Her statement made my temples pulse.

"You're just a girl?"

"What I mean is, what is a girl supposed to do to teach empathy to a bunch of knucklehead boys?"

"Ha!" *Empathy*. "I believe that's the right question to ask, Tilly. Let's think of what you could do."

She contemplated, scrunching up her nose and squinting her eyes.

"Um, I might talk to Miss Harris about wrapping up their legs."

"Go on."

"Well, if we wrap them up tight and make them run a relay race like that, maybe then they'll see how it feels to lose their natural stride. Maybe then they'll show empathy."

"From where did you hear that word, empathy? For being

just a girl, you understand the context of the term better than most adults."

"Mother Theodore explained it to us in our religious studies class. I liked the idea."

"Well, my young genius, I think you have a plan, and I can't wait to hear how things go." She smiled. "Better?"

"Better, Mama."

That night, when I got on my knees to pray, I asked the Lord for more empathy in the world. It made sense, and it came from the mouth of an innocent, from the heart of *just a girl*. I then thought of Will, and next came the sounds of a hacking croup coming from George's room.

CHAPTER 24

George lay asleep on my lap, finally. He had had a bad day, and I feared his influenza-like symptoms would turn to pneumonia, especially when his fever spiked. For hours I changed the cool rags, strategically placed around his wrists, knees, and ankles while running my fingers through his thick brown locks. For more than a decade we tried to prevent sickness, knowing that the slightest wheeze could turn deadly when exposed to threatening elements. It would still be some time before the doctor arrived, so I was keeping close watch on the ailing child until Junior knocked.

"Johanna has the sickness, too," he whispered, noticing George's closed eyes. "I went to check on Tilly before going to work, and though she's fast asleep, Johanna was tossing and turning on the other side of the room."

"Did you speak to her?" I asked. "Is she awake?"

"I think she's delirious," he replied. "She's saying something about going to a morgue. I can hardly understand her because she's muttering in German."

Ever since Father's passing, Mother never spoke German. She enjoyed the kids referring to her as Oma as well as Grandma, but she dedicated herself to English conversation only, saying it was best for Tilly to be immersed in the language necessary to excel in her studies. And George had enough to deal with, without further confusion of two languages in the house. So, when Junior heard Mother muttering in her native tongue, spurting indecipherable words with a horrific tone, he told me that he attempted to calm her, but his touch could not pacify her.

"Her eyes are wild, and when I brushed away sweaty strands from her forehead, I realized that she was burning up."

I immediately eased George away from me and placed his tired body on the bed. I went into the next room, finding Mother covered in blankets, and her pleas of "no morgue" echoing off the walls.

"Mother, it's Livia. Everything is okay. No one is going to the morgue."

No morgue? I remembered Mother being heartsick when hearing about Chicago's abandoned fire victims. With no one to claim their bodies, they were sent to a morgue on Milwaukee Avenue and eventually put to rest somewhere on the outskirts of the city—their forgotten hearts buried alone, their souls invisible. But what was making Mother think of these things now?

"Sie nehmen ihn! Beeilen Sie sich! Rette ihn! Nr. Leichenschauhaus! Er hat einen Namen! Sagen Sie ihnen, seinen Namen!" ("They will take him! Hurry! Save him! No morgue! He has a name! Tell them his name!")

Junior came in with fresh rags, and we started removing the colorful blankets, the mismatched yarns knitted together by Mother when her sight was weak but her fingers still skillful. She fought us while shivering with fever and accused us of trying to kill her. After some coaxing and a bit of tea, she calmed enough to allow me to sit behind her and hold her the way I did George, stroking her face with the soft and cool cloth, hoping that the doctor was on his way.

"This doesn't look good," said Junior, staring down at Mother's shin as he lifted her foot.

It was a rash of reddish pox, a small group of them dotting a line up her leg. My heart pounded, pondering the imminent affliction.

CHAPTER 25

The green fields came to a halt by a short wall of golden leaves swaying in the autumn breeze. The barn was there, built of logs stacked straight and sturdy, and as the scene before me came into focus, I could make out the open doors. The heaps of curing, amber foliage, already cut and staked on poles, were lying in wait to be bundled and strung from the interior roof. The aroma of fresh tobacco came wafting across the field, and then they appeared. Four ruddy-complected men—almost identical in height and build, and clad in overalls and boots— were standing just west of the shelter, cigars hanging from their lips. They caught my sight, and I was transfixed by their eyes, so blue and clear and happy.

"George!"

The voice was shouted from behind me, from the frame home down the path. She ran out the door, across the porch, down the steps, and I saw George struggling to get up. He was smiling from ear to ear, and what a breathtaking sight it was to witness the precious boy lifting himself up and turning his head toward Catherine. His feet were bare, and he looked down at his toes pressed firmly upon the dirt, his arches and heels feeling the soft soil.

"George!" He turned to her summons—he heard her! Her arms were wide, and her dress was flowing. Oh, she was radiant! "Go ahead, George, go!" I coaxed him. And he took a step, and then another, and then trotting, galloping even, through the grass and through the crops until they embraced in a glow of

light. The four men joined the joyous reunion, and then all six figures stopped and turned in my direction, but they were not looking at me, rather above me, waving and smiling, and I felt a gust of cool air rush through my veins, causing every hair on my body to stand on end. A brilliant illumination gracefully fluttered across my shoulder, along my elbow, and squeezed my hand. I thought I heard her words, soft and sweet: "Ich liebe Sie meine Tochter, meine schöne Tochter." (I love you my daughter, my beautiful daughter.)

"MOTHER!"

Franz jumped. "What in God's name are you dreaming about now, Livia?"

"We have to get to the sick house," I said, frantically searching for my shoes.

"They won't let you in. We tried on the way home from the cemetery. They said she was improving, but we still couldn't see her."

"Stay if you want, but I'm going to the sick house. She has taken a turn. I have to be there for her." My voice was calm, but my insides shook with dread.

"Stop it, Livia. You're being irrational." I shot a glare through the darkness, and then Franz sighed. "You're still in mourning over George. We just buried the poor child a day ago. Your dream, at least your dream tonight, is perhaps logical, but we were told just yesterday—"

"George ran to Catherine in my dream. Your father, my father, and Uncle George were waiting for him. Jonas, too." I

185

held my work shoes and dress in my arms, the dress that Mother had made for me just before her eyesight went for good. "The doctors took George away from us, and he was alone when he died. Franz, he was suffering from the smallpox; he was in discomfort and pain, and no one was with him. My God, I wasn't with him!"

"All the smallpox patients are under quarantine, Liv. There's nothing anyone can do about this epidemic except hope that their friends and relatives live through it. Your mother survived and is on her way to recovery. They told us yesterday."

"My dream says otherwise." I turned and left the room.

CHAPTER 26

"I'm checking on Johanna Haas. She's my mother."

The hospital, a morose structure, was a twin to the jailhouse with its boxlike form and barred windows. Upon entering the wooden doors, even the healthy visitor was sickened by the dingy walls and dull decor, the mixed aromas of vinegar and excrement. The employees wore masks for reasons that went beyond the risk of contracting disease.

"There's been no change," said the desk attendant, a dark haired woman whose cap hugged the tight bun on her head. She didn't look up from her clipboard, nor did she acknowledge my presence with more than those four words.

I tapped the table between us. "How do you know?" I asked. "You haven't looked at her file; you haven't inquired about her status."

Without even a tilt of her face, she mumbled from behind her mouth cloth, "There have been no reports, ma'am."

"What is that supposed to mean?" I demanded, but she remained silent as she vigilantly continued to fill out the forms in front of her. "I am asking about my mother, Johanna Haas. She was admitted several days ago, diagnosed with small pox." Still no response. Leaning in close so that my nose practically met her forehead, I spoke in as controlled a voice as I could muster. "I lost my boy from the same disease. I am worn and angry and bitter, and I'm telling you this as a warning, that I have no patience with insolence, even if that's not your intent."

Her swarthy eyes lifted momentarily. "It means that there

have been no additions to the release list and no additions to the deceased list." She returned her gaze to the papers. "There's been no change."

My palms slammed the tabletop, causing her clipboard to bounce and her face to lose color, but before either of us could speak, two hands took hold of my shoulders.

"Livia." His warm breath made me shiver, and I thought for a moment that I had yet to awaken from my earlier dream. "Step outside with me, eh."

The picnic flashed into my head with Catherine standing at my side and Will's presence stunning me into silence. I allowed him to lead me toward the door and through it, into the dawn that was approaching the city.

"Am I dreaming?" I asked, walking by his side along the hospital's short stone path.

"No, Liv. This is real. I'm alive."

"But the obituary said—"

"It was Da who succumbed to the flames. William Magee, Sr."

He motioned for me to sit on a bench. I sat, as he did, and our knees touched slightly.

"For whom are you here?"

"Mother," I replied. "And you?"

"Margaret." He looked away.

"Charlie's Margaret?"

Time had aged him some with silver strands mixing with his brown waves, still full-headed, though, with those memorable simple lines dancing from the corners of his eyes into his temples.

Will cleared his throat before responding, and he placed his hand on mine. "Charlie left the carpentry business, ya see. He became a fireman and saved more lives than I know. Each breathing body he pulled from a burning structure was symbolic of the act he wished he could have performed on our da. It's a noble profession, eh, and me brother died a hero." He stopped talking and squeezed my hand. "When Charlie passed away—" He stopped again and looked away. "It's customary for the brother to wed the widow." This time his words came out quickly.

"I see." I straightened my back and moved my knee away from his. "So, that was Margaret and you at the eight-hour day meeting? I saw you."

Will nodded. "I saw you, too, Liv, and my heart stopped beating, eh?"

"Charlie's Margaret and you?"

He nodded again.

"Since when does Will Magee follow customary protocol?"

"Since I let go." We were silent for what felt like an eternity. "I've come to realize that life is bigger than you and me. There are children and families, people who are affected by our words and actions. Sometimes sacrifice is not negotiable, Liv. And my sacrifice is you."

"Did you ever wonder?"

"After the fire, I came searching for you, got into a fight or two with the guardsmen who were blocking the North."

"I remember when Sheridan was called in."

"Wasn't the Irishman from the south side not allowed over, eh? But I did get across after a time, and I made it into your neighborhood only to find it burnt out." His foot ground a rock into the gravel. "St. Michael's still stood, and I wandered there a bit, but I didn't stay long. I couldn't."

I pictured Will walking aimlessly, all the while I was away at The Sisters of Charity Home.

"Do you know that I married, too?"

"Yes, Liv."

"I had no option. Catherine died in the fire, and I—"

"I know."

"You know?"

"I know that Catherine perished and her baby survived. I learned about your family's fate shortly after I got back from New York. When Da died in the fire, me ma went back east to be with her sisters, and I saw to her needs until she died." He leaned back on the bench. "I understand your circumstances."

"You understand nothing, Will."

"Franz is a fine man. I've prayed for you. That he's been good to you."

"How can you say that *you've* been praying for *me* when *I'm* the one who's been praying, Will? *I'm* the one who's been lost in believing your death. How could you not come for me?"

"It hurts to see you, Liv," he said, his eyes catching mine, locked.

"And it hasn't hurt me every minute of every day? Replaying in my dreams your words, your eyes, your voice, your touch. My God, Will! I've been tortured, and I cannot believe

190

that you allowed this to happen to me. I thought you loved me."

"Don't do this, Livia."

Will leaned forward on the bench, his elbows resting on his knees and head bending down into his calloused hands.

"What am I doing but being honest with you? You want me to lie? To say, 'Well, it was nice seeing you, Will. We had a good time of it years ago, eh?'" I rose on the last word. "Is that what I'm supposed to do?"

He stood and grabbed my arms, pulled me close without our bodies touching.

"You think you're the only one who has suffered? Is that it, Liv?" he asked with a shake of his grasp. "That it didn't kill me inside when I found out you married Franz, started a family? I understood. I did. I still do, but my world fell apart." He paused, released his hold, and stepped back from me. "I thought the only way to ease the pain was to get you off my mind, but I couldn't. The connection was too strong, the desire too great. That's why I didn't come for you, why I had to let you go."

"With no contact, no discussion, as if I had no say in how this would all turn out. You didn't want my input?"

"Input? What choice did we have? Our separation was not my decision. This is what life handed us, no fault of yours or mine."

Will's hands reached into his jacket pockets. His right emerged with a flat rock which he balanced on his palm, while his left hand lifted with rose-worn beads weaving between his fingertips. My own hands cupped my mouth with a gasp.

"We're relocating to Wisconsin, near Margaret's family. In

hopes that it will help her healing." He said. "Before I leave, I could give this back, but wouldn't I prefer—" he started.

"Don't," I reprimanded. "Don't you dare honor me with keeping my rosary all this time and then offend me by offering to return it."

His squint pulled at my heartstrings.

"Take this then, will ya," he said and handed me the rock. "I call it my worry stone, a piece I picked up in the debris of St. Michael."

I took the gift and rubbed it as Will did just moments earlier. "It reminds me to have strength, to wake up even when I don't want to, eh? To live."

I smiled. "Thank you, Will." Another moment of silence lingered between us as I stared at the stone. "You know, for years I've been asking *what if,* wondering what could have been."

"I can't do that, Liv. You shouldn't either."

"I know. I'm supposed to just forget."

"Nah, Liv. We'll never forget."

"Then what?"

"We let go."

"This isn't fair." I balled the stone into a fist and brought it to my heart. "Every day I long for night, for sleep. Others think it's because of fatigue, but it's not. When I close my eyes, you come back to me." I took a deep breath. "There's a lot you need to know."

He took my fist and lifted it to his lips. "And if you never saw me, I'd never know the difference." He kissed my knuckles;

my knees nearly buckled.

"How sad this all is."

"I wish life was different," he whispered and then drew me into his chest. "I still love you, Livia. I always will."

Behind us the main doors of the hospital creaked, and the call of my name stopped time. "Mrs. Dietz? Mrs. Dietz, we have a new report!"

CHAPTER 27

Will's resurgence and disappearance coupled with Mother's coffin descending into the earth next to George created a volcano of sorrow on the brink of explosion.

"Ecclesiastes 3:1-2," the priest said. "For everything there is a season, and a time for every matter under heaven: a time to be born, and a time to die; a time to plant, and a time to pluck up what is planted." With those words, the last shovel of dirt rained on her eternal bed, and I clenched a fist around my stone. Mrs. Heinrich's pat on the back was no consolation, and I allowed Junior to comfort Tilly, for he had a tenderness about him, a tenderness that had turned to temporary hardness in my own heart. Franz never made it to the service because his boss refused the time off, and Franz didn't argue about it. No one argued. Ever. No one talked back; no one stood up. *Won't I forever encourage the questioning of mere men.*

"Oh, Livia, I'm sorry for your loss and for intruding on you at this time." The voice was that of Sarah from the sewing factory. She hugged a thin jacket around herself. "But I'm afraid that, if you don't get back to work, immediately, you'll be let go." *We let go.*

I marched out the cemetery's iron gateway, through the city streets with wind stinging my cheeks, and I returned to my chair. A basketful of cuffs sat there in addition to the regular load of stitching assignments on my table.

"What is this?" I demanded of the girl at the next machine. Her youthful face glanced at me in horror, wide-eyed and pale white, immobilized. She only gave a nod and returned to her work. "What?" I asked.

The girl's source of fear poked at my back. "Is there a problem?" The pin-striped pants and bowler hat gave the appearance of more height than there actually was.

"My problem is this basket," I announced, glaring straight into his narrowed expression. "Cuffs are not my responsibility. They never have been."

"The cuffs are on your chair."

"Yes. And as I said, cuffs are not—"

"I shouldn't have to repeat myself, but I will make exception this one time. The cuffs are on your chair; therefore, they are your responsibility. Another word and your job will be on the line." He fingered his watch and chain, checked the time, turned and walked toward the staircase.

"My job was on the line the moment I applied years ago. Everyone's job is on the line everyday," I stated. He continued his sauntering step without recognition of my voice. "I don't know how you look in the mirror, Mr Jensen," I admonished him, and he stopped on the landing. "Are you a God-fearing man, Mr. Jensen?" I called out.

"Not that it is any of your business, woman, but I'll have you know that I donate more money to my church than you'll ever see in a lifetime. Now get to work!"

"You seem to misunderstand me, Mr. Jensen!" I hollered. "I asked if *you* fear *God*. I did not ask to whom you *instill* fear, like your church's leadership through bribery, like every woman in this factory through threats."

195

"You're fired, woman! Leave the premises immediately, or I will have you escorted out!"

"It's Livia, Mr. Jensen! I have a name, and it is Livia!" I picked up the basket and threw it to the ground. "And mark my word, man, that if you didn't fear God before this day, you'd better have a change of heart!" He waved a worker over and pointed at me. "I hope you hang a few more mirrors in that mansion of yours, and I hope you see my reflection every time you walk past! You have no soul! You have no sense of humanity!"

"Security!"

"What if you were burying your own mother, Mr. Jensen! Would you be fit to work? When your wife falls dead, will you expect your daughter to slave at a machine for you?"

"On Being Afraid"
Written by Miss Anonymity

Of what are we afraid? Unemployment? As if our present employers are worthy of our service! As if we won't survive without the pittance we are given! We throw away our children and families in order to provide for men who deem us as nothing more than slaves to their fortunes! Of what are we afraid? Stained images? Look at the blemishes of he who has the gall to scar our names! I see them! And this is why he can not look into a mirror, for fear of seeing them himself! Our Lord sees them! And this is why he attends church—he hears nothing and believes nothing and doesn't even pray for forgiveness. No, he is there in God's presence to alleviate his own scarred image! Pompous and proud!

What do we do with this fear? What ammunition do we, the humble and poor, have against the powerful elite who own every part of our daily lives, who own US? They have us by the bootstraps, but cowering is no longer an option. Through our fear we only aggravate the condition, becoming indirect accomplices to the corruption. Each time we lower our heads and turn away, we allow the establishment to continue their cruelties, and they use our silence as their protection. We are their victims, and we are their shields!

Where is our leverage? I will tell you what we have that they do not . . . NUMBERS! Our army is so much greater!

Do you recall the reciprocal fear in '71, when our city burned to ashes, when money and property were non-existent, and for a moment we were all homeless paupers together? Do you remember walking shoulder-to-shoulder with them? In our view, we felt mercy and pitied them and helped them; in their view, they were afraid, so utterly afraid that they summoned the National Guard to divide us immediately! There was no reason for this action; even the military and political leaders said so, but our numbers were too great, and the threat of movement within the classes, or by God, losing the class system all together, was too much to bear. The mere thought of standing at our side instead of above us, the mere thought of equality was beyond them.

Over and over again I've been told that now is not the time to take a stand. I started thinking that way myself because of fear – fear of betraying my husband, my coworkers, even my bosses! But our willingness to remain idle, to not get involved, betrays the people who we hold most dear, our children. By not standing up now, we are simply waiting for our children to become the next generation of victims who will have to make these decisions for themselves. Don't you see? We are foisting our workplace problems onto them, when we have the power of numbers today! Oh, don't let the bourgeois propaganda instill anymore fear into you! Don't let their words of hatred, their threats of anarchy evils and atheist agendas fool you! I am a Christian woman who truly believes that

Jesus would be walking with us if we chose to boycott or strike. He is one of us. He is within us. I do not call for violence; I do not call for taking up arms. But I do urge a wake up call – a call for our troops, the workers, to listen up and stand up! Together, and only together, can we fight with the only weapons necessary—our NUMBERS!

CHAPTER 28

"You are *not* going back to that office. I forbid it," declared Franz.

"I beg your pardon," I replied.

"You heard me. It was a blessing when the Parsons were evicted. After months of reassuring my bosses that the Parsons were merely neighbors by circumstance and not by choice, the questioning ceased when that couple moved away, and now my own wife's seeking them out and conspiring with the whole lot of 'em!" He waved a folded newspaper in the air. "This is preposterous, Livia. What's going on in your head? Why would you want to be in contact with those people?" The paper was whipped into the garbage can.

It was already nighttime when Franz had stormed in the back door and started his inquisition. His hollering brought Mrs. Heinrich, who had come to live with us soon after Mother passed, tiptoeing from the second bedroom with a shushing finger over her lips. Franz snapped at her with an expression of contempt, and she retreated back into the room.

"Contrary to your belief, Franz," I whispered, modeling the voice level I wished he would use with Tilly and Mrs. Heinrich already set for bed, "the Parsons were, and still are, my friends. When I lost my job at the sewing factory, Lucy was livid and supported me completely, unlike your self-absorbed reaction to how my dismissal was going to affect *you*."

"Self-absorbed?" he yelled.

"The Parsons encouraged me to share my story instead of

keeping silent, and when I wrote about my experience, they ran it as an anonymous opinion piece. The readership responded, and so I felt compelled to continue writing." It felt good having it off my chest and out in the open. Being secretive with Franz was not my favorite option, but it was my only option if I wanted to stay on at the paper.

"Behind my back?" he asked.

"Yes, Franz, behind your back because I knew how you would react." I took a deep breath and then continued. "I'm a good writer, Franz. I have things to say, and people are listening."

"Yeah, they're listening. All the men at the factory have big ears and bigger mouths when they talk about this anonymous writer. They say she's asking a lot of questions, questions that could be dangerous to her family, and they're debating as to what they would do if they found out that "Miss Anonymity" was their own wife. When Josef passed me the latest paper, and I read the article, I knew it was you. I just knew it!"

"Don't you see, Franz, they're reading my words, and they're listening to truths. An ordinary wife and mother like me doesn't have a political agenda. I simply write and question about my own life and thoughts. The truth can, indeed, be dangerous, I understand, but if enough people hear me— "

The back door opened, and Junior walked in from his late shift.

"I'll show you one reader who is NOT listening, and that's me! You are not a journalist, Livia, and I'm saying right here and now that I forbid your association with these anarchists.

You're asking for trouble. I could lose my position again, and excuse me if I sound *self-absorbed*, but my income is necessary for ALL of us, not just myself!"

"So I guess he found out, then," said Junior as he grabbed a glass from the cupboard and poured himself some water.

"He knows about this?" Franz asked vehemently.

"Yes," I replied.

"Who else? Who else knows about this?"

Mrs. Heinrich quietly reemerged from the bedroom, closing the door gently behind her until she heard the light click of the knob settling into the frame.

"Does she know, too?" Franz demanded while pointing at our tenant.

"Yes," I replied again.

"For God's sake, am I a stranger in my own home?" he boomed loudly and pounded his fist on the table, making the plates that were still left from supper jump in unison, startling all of us in the room.

"Father, she has a gift," Junior interjected, and Franz's glassy eyed glare narrowed in on his son.

"You have no business in this discussion! This is MY home, and MY decision, and I'll say it one last time!" He turned to me and pointed with vulgar passion. "I forbid your association with those anarchists!"

Being enlightened of my close association with the Parsons vexed him, and I felt Franz's agitation growing deeper in his less-than-sober state of mind. His breathing was loud, his eyes fixed on me like the night he declared me a whore. "We'll talk

202

about this tomorrow when you are more civil," I said calmly, and I started gathering the dirty tableware.

My last statement triggered Franz's anger to the point of swiping his hand across the table. We were in stunned shock at the sound of shattering plates and glass and the revolting look in Franz's eyes.

"Father, you're acting like a madman!" yelled Junior, as he grabbed his father's shoulder to encourage a greater distance between him and me. Simultaneously, Tilly started wailing from the next room, and I ran to her while Mrs. Heinrich bent down to retrieve pieces of shattered dishes. Franz threw back his fist and swung a blow to Junior's face that brought the young man crashing into the basin. Blood from his jaw turned the porcelain tub to red, and Franz froze, his hand still balled up tightly, white-knuckled and all.

With Tilly clutching my waist, I witnessed Mrs. Heinrich's horrified expression as Junior pushed past his father and walked out, holding his mouth and leaving a trail of crimson droplets on the ground.

"Junior!" I called, but the only response was the slam of the screen door.

"What have you done!" I yelled to Franz, while Tilly cried and shook like a leaf.

He didn't argue. As if trying to wash off his drunkenness and wash away the entire episode, Franz leaned over the basin and splashed water on his face and hands.

"Mrs. Heinrich, take Tilly back to bed," he said flatly, drying his fingers on a towel.

The woman set the broken pieces on the counter and took my girl into her own arms. I gave Tilly a kiss on the cheek and told her I would tend to her soon, and just as they were about to exit, Mrs. Heinrich turned toward Franz.

"I'm not one to get involved with family matters," she began, "and I don't mean any disrespect to you, Franz, as I am eternally grateful that you have welcomed me into your home, but Johanna and Otto would not approve of your behavior tonight, and for them I feel it my responsibility to tell you so."

Franz wiped his face and looked directly at the woman. "They wouldn't approve of their daughter associating with anarchists, either."

"Quite the opposite, Franz, I think they'd be very proud. You obviously didn't know the Haas family like I did."

Franz threw down the towel and stormed out.

Mrs. Heinrich went into the bedroom with Tilly.

I collapsed into a chair, letting my head fall on to the barren table surface, and I wept. *My God! Where are you?*

CHAPTER 29

"That is not a nice word, Mama," Tilly retorted while crossing her arms.

"No, sweetheart," I agreed, "it is not a nice word."

At age twelve, Tilly was already showing signs of activism. On this occasion, she was voicing her disapproval of the language used by Mrs. Blooman, a racist character in the story of *The Three Pine Trees* by Jacob Abbot, a book we had checked out at the local library earlier in the day. Mrs. Blooman boasted, "For if there is any thing in the world that I absolutely hate, it is a nigger."

"Some of my classmates talk like that, and when I tell them they shouldn't speak that way, they say I don't know anything because I never spoke to a colored child, and if I had, I'd know that they were niggers."

"And how do you respond to that?" I inquired.

"Well," she started thoughtfully, inching closer to me on her bed, "colored children don't go to the same schools as me and might not learn to read and write like me. That's probably why they talk different. They don't have our vocabulary."

You know what I'm thinking when you talk that way, don't you, Jonas?

"That's very observant, Tilly. I'm proud of you."

"Do you know any colored people, Mama?"

"I do. Our former neighbor, Lucy Parsons, is part Negro, and a long time ago I worked at a hotel with a lady named Clementine." I smiled at the thought of her. "She was a wonderful friend."

"Do you see her anymore?"

"Unfortunately, Tilly, I don't know what became of her. We lost touch after the hotel burned down in the great fire. I've prayed for her many nights, hoping that she survived and that life has been good to her."

"I don't like Mrs. Blooman. I prefer Old Uncle Giles who says to 'never call a boy by any name you think he don't like.' Even though poor Rainbow didn't say anything about it, he didn't want to be called that name, and I'm sure he was mad on the inside."

Only true friends are allowed to call me bys my real name.

"It's getting late, my love. I need to get up early for my first day at Dieter's Tailor Shop, so how about we pick up again tomorrow night?"

"No, Mama!" she pleaded. "We can't do that. You can't possibly stop with that insulting word lingering in my head. Let's read on, so we can get to a different scene for me to think about before I go to sleep."

"Shall we recite some poetry instead? Some Whitman or Thoreau, maybe?" I asked, thinking that Rainbow's next scene might be just as bothersome as the last.

"Ooh, yes!" she exclaimed. "Or maybe Poe's 'Annabel Lee!'"

"That's a sad one, sweetheart. How about something more uplifting."

"Oh, no, Mama! Annabel Lee is beautiful, and her love is so beautiful that even the angels see it! I want to recite this one and drift off listening to the sound of the sea."

Tilly fetched the poetry book, and after paging through the text, she stopped and looked at me with sad eyes.

"Mama, I miss George."

"I miss him, too, my love."

"And I miss Oma Johanna, too."

I leaned in so that our foreheads touched.

"I miss her, too."

"Sometimes, I think about acting out stories for George or playing hide and seek with Oma, and I smile at the memories."

"Well, those are good thoughts, aren't they?"

"Yes, but then my stomach gets all crunched up because I miss them so much it hurts."

I placed my hands on Tilly's cheeks. Her watery eyes stared up at me, and I wished for words to take away her pain, but I had none, so I turned to Louisa May Alcott: "...for the planting of the acorns was a symbol of the desire budding in those young hearts to be what he might have been, and to make their lives nobler for the knowledge and the love of him." Tilly sat upright, and a grin came across her face.

"Can we plant acorns for George and Oma? Just like the story from *Jack and Jill*?"

"That's exactly what I was thinking."

"That would make them happy."

"Indeed."

After a long hug, Tilly wiped her eyes and returned to the poetry book. She read aloud while my thoughts passed from George to Mother, Father to Jonas, and then to Catherine who talked to me from the other side, and I felt blessed with the strength I gained from the realization that I was never alone.

I nodded off in Tilly's room, beside her in her bed. Memories of Catherine must have continued to dance in my head.

"The Lord asks us to use our gifts, Livia."

"Pardon?"

Catherine's words reached me in a hummed garble, and when I lifted my head from the wash bucket, a strand of hair fell across my brow, cutting her image in two.

"We've been scrubbing floors and clothes for well over an hour, and you've barely spoken. Your gift for gab is something I tend to enjoy."

"I'm sorry Catherine," I responded while using my sleeve to wipe my face and push back my hair. "I'm a bit preoccupied."

"With thoughts of Jonas?" she inquired.

I nodded and fought back the tears.

"Come sit down and talk with me." She pulled two chairs over the damp wooden floorboards and motioned for me to join her.

"We need to get this finished," I said, frozen on my knees, unwilling to let down my defenses. "We mustn't waste any precious time while Junior is napping." I turned back to the bucket and dunked my rag.

"We're entitled to a break, especially when such sorrow is weighing on our hearts. I worry about Jonas, too, as much as I worry about Franz."

"Which is precisely why I refrain from sharing my thoughts with you, Catherine. There's nothing I'm going through with my brother that you haven't already endured for the last two years with your husband. I know you understand me, but my bleak conversation would only add to your own distress, and I care about you too much to do that."

"Livia Haas, you have reached out to comfort me each day Franz has been gone." She stood. "Your readings while I nurse Junior to sleep are welcomed distractions to give my tension reprieve. You lend me an ear, offer a prayer, pick up my chores when I can't manage to pick up my head in the morning. You entertain my child so I can write to my husband in peace. Shall I go on?"

"There's no need."

"Well then, talk to me. Give me an opportunity to be there for you, too."

Tossing my rag to the side I blurted, "What's to say that you already don't know? My heart races, my stomach clenches, I have no appetite and can't sleep, and I'm afraid, Catherine, I'm —" The flood gates opened to a river of tears as my body shook, earthquake tremors, violent and hysterical, uncontrollable.

"Oh, my poor girl, I know. I know." Catherine rushed over, enveloped me in her arms, and in that embrace we remained for some time, two bodies like two hands prayerfully entwined, molding our sisterhood into a permanent, forever force.

"I have something for you," Catherine whispered as we slowly released each other, patting wet faces with our aprons.

"What for?" I asked.

"It's just a little something to engage your thoughts. A gently used collection of Edgar Allen Poe."

Before I could muster words to express my gratitude, Mother's voice boomed from the front porch. "They're here!"

"Who's here?" I asked my friend just as I felt the energy radiating from her body and pulling her toward the door. I rushed to follow, both of us in our stocking feet, grabbing shawls off the rack as we exited. I was still clutching the book.

Catherine sprinted to meet the buggy, as I approached Mother and asked what was happening.

"One of the field hands brought news before sunrise," she responded. "A soldier came walking into town late last night. Mr. Foulke gave him a bed. The soldier was named Franz."

"And father went for him?"

"Immediately."

"Without telling Catherine?"

Mother gave a slight glare in my direction. "And what if it wasn't our Franz after all? Why would we raise hopes?"

"True enough," I said.

But it was Franz, indeed, wearing his torn and dirty uniform and looking disheveled from head to toe. Catherine was holding him with splayed fingers across his lower back, her head buried upon his chest. Rays of sunlight poured through cloud crevices onto their bodies now pulsing like a single heartbeat, heaving sobs of joy, of relief. Franz was home, and the image of this jubilant reunion brought to mind our Blessed Mother, how she must have reacted to seeing her only son the first time after he rose from the dead.

Praise God! Franz was home!

I was startled awake by the slamming door. I heard his shoes shuffling through the kitchen, a chair screeching across the floor and then banging into something, the table maybe. Indeed. Franz was home.

CHAPTER 30

The tavern was nondescript from the walkway, a structure sandwiched between a tenement building and piano factory. "Rainer's" was painted across the entrance, the uneven title announced in a beige tint. I took a deep breath and straightened my posture before touching the door handle.

A light smoky mist veiled the room with the scent of tobacco wafting in my direction. Several patrons were sprinkled throughout the scene, solitary figures taking up space at lonely round tables or along the wooden surface that stood parallel to the the side wall. Dim candles made it difficult to see the drinker from his shadow at each spot.

Organizing the bottle shelves behind the counter, Rainer's hands turned the rum labels to face forward. Rounded shoulders made him appear shorter than I remembered from our picnic days, and when he heard my shoes tap on the hard floor, his neck twisted to see who entered. Beneath bushy brows of white, his large cloudy blues met my attention.

"Livia, dear." His quivering voice showed aging, as did the contrast between his deep pink scalp and thinned powdery hair which brought out the brown spots dotted along the temples. He cleared his throat and asked, "How's Franz doing?"

"That's precisely why I'm here, Rainer. You cannot serve him anymore. His body can't take it."

No one turned toward me. No one even looked up from the spirits held in their hands.

"Life is hard, Livia. I know it's difficult for you, having to

212

deal with Franz's stubborn ways and frequent absence. But he finds peace here."

"He finds peace in a drink that briefly dulls reality, but eventually he wakes to find himself in the same place with the same circumstances." I sat down on an open stool to get closer. "Rainer, there's no peace for one's health when his insides are dying. The alcohol is destroying him."

"That depends on how you define 'insides.'" A tapping vibrated beneath my palms. He wiped the bar top with a damp rag and held his pointer finger to a man at the end of the counter. "I'll be there in one minute, Jack."

Leaning in, Rainer whispered. "Life destroyed his soul a long time ago, and the soul is the 'inside' part that I deal with at this establishment." He reached under the counter and retrieved an empty tumbler. "Rest assured, I do cut off Franz," he said, "but I can't, however, stop him from moving on to another tavern." He cleared his throat again, and without so much as a glance at the crystal cube he dropped into the cup, he continued to preach as he stirred water to dissolve the sugar. "George's death put him over the edge. With no disrespect to you Liv, each day that child lived, Franz felt like he was doing something right by his first wife." Rainer took two bottles from the cramped shelves of clear and brown glass. One was a rye whiskey, and had I not been able to read the tag, I would have identified the dark amber liquid by its sweet aroma as he measured it into a jigger and set it aside. "I'm not a doctor, so a drink and an ear is the only medicine I've got for sorrowful men." He turned his head to cough and then opened the second bottle, the bitters. I caught its earthen scent and watched Rainer put several dashes into the concoction, grab a piece of ice and lemon peel, and mix with his right hand while adding the whiskey with his left. "I can't make any promises, Livia. Every man has his own lines to live with, and only *he* knows when he needs to cross one to find peace."

I never thought of Franz as having lines, but I recognized my own, and there was truth to what Rainer said. He lifted the glass and headed toward his patient patron. I stared at his easy stride, the way he proudly set down the drink as if presenting a gift. I listened to the soothing way he asked the man how life was treating him. Rainer's elbows rested on the bar with hands clasped, and his eyes peered intently as he nodded to the response. "A man's character is defined not by someone else's opinion of him, but how he reacts to those opinions," he told the man. With a pat on the shoulder, he concluded, "Stay strong, my friend."

I motioned to the bartender. "Yes, Liv?"

"What was that drink?"

"An old-fashioned."

"I'd like to try it. Maybe just a half glass."

Rainer smiled and reached for another tumbler. "This one's on the house."

CHAPTER 31

I had just arrived at the *Alarm* office, and Lucy was up in arms about a raid that had taken place the night before. Apparently, Albert's friend, a socialist and movement leader by the name of August Spies, was leery of a newcomer who was in attendance at a meeting to discuss an upcoming demonstration. "Could he be an undercover policeman?" Albert asked his colleague, but before August could respond, two dozen officers barreled through every door and window of the restaurant in which they were gathered. "Everyone was arrested. They had no grounds! They had no right!" Lucy declared.

"What did he look like?" I asked. "The undercover policeman – did anyone say anything about him?"

"He was a large man with a heavy German accent. Albert said that more than his voice, it was his eyes that gave him away. It was his expression, the deep anger that made his taunting eyes twitch making August feel uncomfortable, like there was something sinister and untrustworthy about him."

My heart sank, and I instantly ran home to check on my family. When I approached, the scene at the apartment was frenzied. Before setting foot on the back staircase, Junior came flying down the steps with two buckets.

"Junior! What in heaven's name is going on up there?" I inquired with apprehension.

"It's Father. Mrs. Heinrich sent for me." He was speaking in spurts of sentences, out of breath. "He's throwing up. Bad. Throwing up blood."

"Did someone send for the doctor?"

"He refuses. I said I was going to take care of the buckets. But I'm going to fetch the doctor right now. He'll hate me, but I figured he already does."

"No, Junior, your father does not hate you. He hates himself." I took a deep sigh and quickly hugged him. "Go now. Go and get the doctor, and I'll take care of fresh water."

I wasn't prepared to see him. I'd witnessed the young and vibrant Franz while working the tobacco fields, sweat beads rolling along his forehead and temples, affectionate eyes as green and fresh as the hills around him. I'd witnessed his tender side with Catherine when his arms held her close, powerful and enchanting at the same time. I'd witnessed Franz's depressed and bitter states with tight lips and reddened gaze of disdain. And I'd witnessed his determined and proud moments, too, with rugged stance and head held high. However, never had I witnessed his pure weakness.

Franz was laid out on the kitchen floor, his head resting on a pile of towels with his face tilted to the side to let the blood flow away from his mouth, colorless lips dried and cracked. The yellow tint of his skin had somehow washed itself away from his face, leaving extreme whiteness behind, settling into the irises, animal-like eyes after being attacked by its predator. His skin felt cold to the touch as I stroked his temple with my thumb. *Oh, Franz.* His glazed eyes met mine in helpless surrender. He attempted a word, but the gurgling red liquid prevented his speech.

He held on long enough for Junior to return with the doctor

who told us it wouldn't do us any good to move Franz; his symptoms were too progressed. It was just a matter of time, and not much at that. One by one we said our good-byes, as tears trickled down his nose and cheek.

Surprisingly, Tilly was composed. She knelt down next to Franz, the only father she ever knew, and brushed his hair away from his forehead, kissing it gently with a soft "I love you," as if he was her doll going to sleep for the night.

Mrs. Heinrich squeezed his hand and made a sign of the cross. She sprinkled holy water and started a rosary.

He looked at me with a searching stare. "I was wrong," he whispered.

"Not now, Franz," I replied.

"I told you to do as you were told." His eyes seemed to look through me, past me, to another place and time. "That's what I said to you." He coughed. "I was wrong."

"You're delirious, Franz. You need to save your strength."

"No. When I went to war. I told you to do as you were told." His speech was strained, his sentences became short. "At some point . . . we must stop . . . following rules . . . and start . . . following our hearts."

"Shhh," I said, placing a finger to his dried lips. I did remember that day when I had to beg Jonas to come and say goodbye to Franz as he left to join the Union. It was a lifetime ago.

Franz appeared just down the path, baggy overalls hanging against his slender build and a tattered hat tilted downward to

217

block the sun, but not so angled to hide his angst-filled eyes gazing upon the infant in his arms and partner at his side. It was difficult to picture the stiff blue jacket that awaited him.

When Franz noticed Jonas sulkily approaching, he handed the baby to Catherine and met my brother at the edge of the road. I saw Franz place his hands on each of Jonas' shoulders, and soon Jonas lifted his face. The two embraced, a robust man-to-man heart-to-heart embrace. My mother wrapped her consoling arms around Catherine and her babe.

Jonas ran off, back toward the barn from which we came, and Franz held out his hand to me. Our farewell was not as dramatic as he pinched my nose and squeezed my fingers. "Keep doing as you're told, Livia," he said to me.

"I will."

"And don't stop all that reading and writing, ya hear?" he smiled.

"Never."

"That's my girl. And you promise to help Catherine, too?" I noticed a slight choking back when he mentioned his wife's name.

"Cross my heart," I said, and I crossed it. He turned.

"God bless you, Franz."

Those were my final words, and with that I let him return to his little family for a few more brief well wishes. Our dear friend threw his bag on to his back and climbed aboard the horse and buggy. Father slapped the animals into gear, and they trotted off, dust forming a curtain of clouds that when lifted, showed only a deserted stage.

His eyes squinted before fluttering. "Keep writing, Liv. Ya hear me." It took everything out of him to finish the sentence. His chest quivered and stomach bounced upward with every labored exhale.

"Cross my heart," I said. And I crossed it. "God bless you, Franz."

Junior was standing back unsure of what to do. I motioned him over to Franz's side, where his father's hand wavered, the slightest movement, in Junior's direction. That gesture was all it took to open the door to his son, to let him know that everything was okay, that he was sorry, that he loved him. Whatever interpretation Junior had of this action, Franz's desire to reach out to his boy was the signal he needed to come forward.

"Be brave, my little man," he whispered.

Franz Dietz took his last breath the same way Junior took his first—together.

Our grassy plot was encircled by cement headstones and marble statues, while my loved ones had nothing to proclaim their births and deaths. Franz joined the others, his simple pine box buried next to Catherine's. I envisioned the words that would have declared him a beloved father and husband.

CHAPTER 32

I was surrounded by yards of red and black and white material, cut into banners with most of the letters sewn and emblems affixed but still needing minor stitch work, when Junior entered the kitchen from the back staircase.

"Getting ready for tomorrow?" he asked.

The next day was Thanksgiving 1884, which was also the day of the Poor People's March organized by Lucy and Lizzie and the International Working People's Association. It felt ironic to be participating in an act of justice on Jonas' birthday.

"Absolutely. I have only a few more stitches to go."

"While you've got your sewing out, could you mend this knee? You wouldn't have to do it tonight if you're too tired." Junior was holding up his torn overalls.

"Of course, I can whip those pants into shape in no time, and while I'm at it, can you get the old pairs from your father's drawer? I never got rid of them, and they might fit you with some mending."

As Junior left to fetch his father's work pants, I called out to him, "Will Mary still be joining us?"

His face peeked around the corner, smiling from ear to ear. "Absolutely."

I met Mary several months prior to the march. She and Sarah came to the newspaper office where I was a volunteer. They wanted to do something, to do their part. They couldn't remain mute forever, they said, but they were afraid of losing their jobs. They asked if we had any discreet responsibilities. I could almost hear Junior's heart skip a beat when the girls entered. Everything about Mary was long and sweet. She had an elongated face with a narrow chin atop an extended neck of smooth skin, creamy pearl. Her piercing teal tinted eyes focused on a speaker, and their words were received with gentility. Though slightly taller than Junior, her presence was never over-powering; rather, she carried herself demurely and spoke quietly through thin lips and a considerate expression. Her fingers were frail, her arms lanky, and when she walked, she had the gracefulness of a dancer with her long legged stride, her skirt floating along the floorboards beneath her. Junior was mesmerized by Mary, and with good reason.

"What's this?" He was grasping a piece of paper found deep in one of Franz's pockets. One side appeared to be a blank prescription form, but the other side had writing. I read the first line, "F.A. 36," Franz's field artillery unit, followed by a list of ten soldier names with the word "DEAD" scrawled next to eight of them, the same death date and location. Franz's name was in the middle of the list, but just the name, nothing else. Then there was the last listing, the name of Karl Faust, and next to his name was a short phrase: "to whom you owe your life." I recognized Karl's writing, and I shook at the sight. It was the same penmanship used in letters to Franz before we came to Chicago. *"Franz must have spoken about everyone at great lengths, because each correspondence mentions the Haas family. Some notes inquire about your parents' well being more than Junior's and mine."* That's what Catherine told me. And that dreadful night of the fire, Karl had said, *"When I saw those papers, his*

221

home in Quakertown, his property owned by a Haas, what choice did I have but to dig at him, find my target—Vati's target?"

Undoubtedly, Karl latched on to Franz because he was connected to our family, the Haas family from Quakertown, Pennsylvania, the family related to George. I returned to the same conclusion I had made in the past; George Haas and Karl's father were enemies. Anything less couldn't possibly instill such need for revenge.

As if he could read my mind, Junior spoke, "He might still be on the force, you know. He could be there tomorrow. Do you still want to walk?"

"Now more than ever, Junior," I said, lifting my head with pure confidence. "Karl would win if I sat back and swallowed my voice out of fear. He has wounded our family enough, and I am ready to face him if the situation presents itself."

At 18th Street between Prairie and Calumet, we gathered at the old cottonwood, a remembrance tree from the battle at Fort Dearborn. Its trunk of an arm extended from the earth with its fingered branches having been lost one by one, and still it continued to reach up to the heavens, stripped of dignity and hope, now barren on this brisk November day. It was a sad tree, and I reflected for a moment on whether or not it was ever hearty and filled with life, a favorite spot for children to play under its cooling shade.

Banners and flags were distributed, and the group grew larger with representation from the I.W.P.A., men and women from every trade and position. As we walked, Mrs. Heinrich and

I were on either side of Tilly.

"Is that a playhouse?" Tilly squeaked with the wonder of a youngster when pointing out the complete log cabin on the Sears' property to our right. We saw two little girls running in and out of its realistic entrance way, full windows with curtains next to the sturdy door, a front porch with a little swing. My child was past handholding and cuddling; tea parties and dandelion picking were a part of our past. However, such a playhouse could not go unnoticed. I hoped Tilly looked back fondly on her childhood, just as I did when I thought of Quakertown, the farm, Haycock Mountain.

Prairie Avenue was pristine and regal. It was home to the city's most influential citizens, originally inhabited by the Pullman and Fields families with fellow powerhouses joining them after the great fire. Extraordinary places were built on the street, one more magnificent than the next. Their mansions were made of limestone and brown stone, redbrick and marble, with exquisite stained glass windows and copper edges, wide terraces and strong pillars. They were designed by famous architects from across the country.

As impressive as they were to the eye, a cloud hovered over the beauty of this magical street when the reality of self-indulgence set in, that nothing seemed to be enough for the owners with their personal conservatories and private libraries, ballrooms and drawing rooms and billiard rooms, even a theater and bowling alley at the Pullman place.

"It was the workingman's toil, sweat, and mistreatment that paid for these decorative whims," I heard a marcher say.

"They've exploited the people on whose backs they achieved their grandeur," another responded.

"Had each business owner implemented the eight-hour day as promised, had they acknowledged the unfair practices that were taking place in their own backyards, they would have avoided discontent among their laborers and employees."

"Father's rolling in his grave," Junior said as he snuck up behind me. "I don't think he'd approve of our participation here."

"I disagree, Junior," I replied. "Not if Catherine is holding him, which I'm sure she is. Your father's at peace, now. I like to think that he always respected my involvement, but he simply succumbed to fear." I smiled. "There's nothing left to fear for Franz."

My hope was that there was nothing to fear for any of us, but I could never be sure.

"When the girl in pink opened the door, I saw real furniture, Mama," Tilly announced. "I think a family could actually live in there!"

CHAPTER 33

Nikolaus held the door for me as I approached the *Alarm* office. "Good to see you, Liv," he said, tipping his cap.

"Thank you, Nikolaus. I don't usually see you during this shift." He was Junior's age and the most intelligent man I knew. Albert and Lucy hired him to work the linotype, a daunting and patient task very few workers could master, but Nikolaus exceeded the Parsons' expectations with a perfectionist's focus.

"Albert sent me a message about a breaking story at the Chicago Board of Trade. I have to set up that hunk of a machine and be ready when he arrives."

"Well, I won't stop you."

"Thanks, Liv. Have a good day."

I heard several ladies in the meeting room where newsletters were being stuffed. Their voices overlapped with details about the rally down at LaSalle and Jackson.

"It ended peaceful? Maybe?" asked Christel, a young helper who was new to the cause, new to the office, new to the country. Her accent didn't prevent understanding.

"When we left, the militiamen had just arrived. They were ordered to force back the protesters," Gitta replied, and then Gitta's mother chimed in.

"From where we could see, I don't think the protesters made it as far as the Board building."

"True, Mother, but I hope their presence put a damper on the festivities."

"I don't understand how these people can participate in

extravagance." Gitta watched her mother push the newsletters to the side and take out a piece of clay, her nimble fingers pulling little sections and molding them into balls and then flattening them into miniature pancakes. "It galls me so!"

Christel stared and asked me, "What she do?"

"That's what Amala does when she's upset. Clay calms her. She's an artist."

"Stick around long enough, Christel, and you'll meet people from all walks of life with all types of skills and gifts. Mother is just one of many talented volunteers."

"Isn't it enough to open the darned building?" Amala asked, oblivious to the artistic praise around her. "But to get elaborate and ceremonial, spending thousands of dollars on a party to pat each others' backs? Especially now, when there's tension and corruption. What are they thinking, these self-professed heroes?" By this time, the clay discs were individually worked into petal forms, pressed into one another to create a rosebud. Gitta stopped stuffing and turned pink in the cheeks.

"It's arrogance and greed," she retorted.

The door flew open. "Where's Niko?" called Albert, his thin frame bolting past us.

"In the linotype room," Amala informed him.

"Good. Has Uwe arrived?"

"Not yet, Albert. Wasn't Uwe at the rally?"

"Yes, but he's supposed to meet me here immediately to put the details together and move it through Niko simultaneously. I want this story out first thing tomorrow morning." As Albert passed a hand through his parted hair, his high forehead appeared. Niko poked his face through the doorway.

"I'm set, Albert. If you want to begin without Uwe, we can do that or wait."

"I'm right behind you, Niko, my man."

Three more volunteers entered with news from the rally, followed by Uwe who we waved into the linotype room. The details were unanimous: confrontations ensued, militia force was used, a bomb was thrown. No one was hurt or killed; no one knew who threw the bomb.

The headlines continued to flow:

MAY 4, 1885: MASSACRE IN LEMONT
—State militia descends on quarry strikers.

That story was followed shortly afterward with:

PINKERTON HIRED TO PROTECT STRIKE BREAKERS
—McCormick Jr. cuts wages after gaining top profits, strikers face the force of detective and his gang.

More and more conflicts made the news, and violence became a common result:

CLUBBING FORCE BY BONFIELD BRINGS INJURY AND IMPRISONMENT TO STREETCAR STRIKERS ON THE CITY'S WEST SIDE.

The streets of Chicago and beyond were experiencing a new kind of war, and there was no denying it. Peaceful demonstrations were antagonized by Detective Pinkerton and

Captain John Bonfield, both loathed public figures, and their aim to induce altercation, as rumor had it, was encouraged and supported by the city's elite.

Junior was working three jobs during this time. He was a member of the Cigar Makers' Union while working in the cigar factory part-time. He was also employed at the lumber yards, until he and his fellow laborers went on strike. To make up for the loss of pay there, he took on nightshift hours at the cemetery whenever he was needed as a gravedigger. He was the hardest worker I knew, and he did all that he was capable of doing to help in the labor movement, too.

Meetings and decisions for every organization in Chicago were getting intense. *The Alarm* became more militant each day, and this divide in my personal principles and the labor movement principles concerned me. I couldn't blame others' brewing hostility, having to face the constant assaults by Pinkerton and Bonfield. The I.W.P.A. was expanding in membership, and the Parsons joined forces with the Knights of Labor, while other factions of socialists, anarchists, and labor unions formed groups demanding more action – strong action. As the fury grew deep, I was caught in the midst of opposing viewpoints: everyone was fighting for the eight-hour day and equality in the workplace, but the problem was in the best way to attain the goal. What was it going to take?

"It's hereditary, dear sister, and the bug will get you, too, mark my word. The only question is whether or not you'll be willing to take arms."

I was secure in my belief about taking arms. At no time, under any circumstances, could I promote violence, and I was not alone in this thinking. Some of the socialists were simply the movers and shakers who could organize and lead this fight, and regardless of their reputation among politicians and mainstream newspapers, I believed individuals like the Parsons to be good people who advocated for a good cause. Unfortunately, we, who were against armed revolts, had a contrary idea to many of the anarchists around us with their increasing resentment and agitation. It was especially contrary to Lucy who gained the distinction of a revolutionary due to her comments in an article she wrote for the *Alarm*. It was called "To Tramps," and it concluded with aggressive advice:

Awaken them from their wanton sport at your expense! Send forth your petition and let them read it by the red glare of destruction. Thus when you cast "one long lingering look behind" you can be assured that you have spoken to these robbers in the only language which they have ever been able to understand, for they have never yet deigned to notice any petition from their slaves that they were not compelled to read by the red glare bursting from the cannon's mouths, or that was not handed to them upon the point of the sword. You need no organization when you make up your mind to present this kind of petition. In fact, an organization would be a detriment to you; but each of you hungry tramps who read these lines, avail yourselves of those little methods of warfare which

Science has placed in the hands of the poor man, and you will become a power in this or any other land.
Learn the use of explosives!

Oh, how I prayed for my friend, whose righteous cause I supported, but whose retaliatory response I opposed! I called upon our Blessed Mother to intercede and bring grace to the movement and into our daily lives.

CHAPTER 34

I thought my prayers were answered when a new priest came to a local church. Father Laurence was a young theologian, charismatic and bold, brash even. His sermons were clever, meaningful, and memorable, but most importantly, his words incited faith and hope in the laborer and offered a Catholic perspective to the workers' plight. In a booming voice from the pulpit, he read from a scripted piece:

It seems that we're always quoting the bible. I remember the way my parents quoted the Good Book, each using the Word of God to suit his and her opinions. When a bully gave me a bloody nose, Father referred to Exodus 21:24, "Eye for eye, tooth for tooth, hand for hand, foot for foot." He told me the Lord would accept my revenge, to go out and give that bully twice the force he gave to me. Mother laughed, "Oh, my son, listen carefully to Matthew 5:38-39 who understood Exodus in a different way. 'You have heard that it was said, Eye for eye, and tooth for tooth. But I tell you, do not resist an evil person. If someone strikes you on the right cheek, turn to him the other also.' I tell you do not provoke another altercation. Walk away the better man." Father would get hot under the collar with Mother's rebuttals and tell her to do as Ephesians 5:22 said, "Wives, submit to your husbands as to the Lord." And Mother would give Father a hug, whispering in her own enjoyment, "Ephesians 5:25 says, 'Husbands, love your wives, just as Christ also loved the church and gave Himself up for her.'" And then she'd kiss him on the cheek and add, "So, I guess we're asked to submit to one another."

I am reminded of these opposing interpretations when I hear the destitute damning the wealthy, "For the love of money is a root of all kinds of evil" and the wealthy condescending the destitute, for "The Lord makes poor and makes rich; he brings low and he exalts." In my mind, if we call ourselves Christian and believe in the true message of Christ, we must follow the biblical passage that has no other translation than what it says: "Do unto others as you would have them do unto you."

Adults have more difficulty with this than children. Let me illustrate my point with a story.

A young lad was sitting in front of the local grocer. He was playing with his jacks when a scruffy boy with an oversized cap and baggy pants came out the door and stopped at the steps, his eyes moving back and forth, back and forth while looking down at a piece of paper. Finally, he crumbled the note and put in his pocket. Feeling the stare of the fine-dressed lad, he asked, "Mind if I sit down?"

"Suit yourself. I'm just waiting for my pa. He's inside picking up a hefty order for Mother's important dinner party tonight."

"Yes, well, my order is here on this paper, and it may not be hefty, but is sure is important."

"If it's so urgent, then why aren't you inside shopping?"

"'Cause I can't read it, and the clerk says he's too busy to help me."

"How old are you?" inquired the lad.

"Ten," replied the scruffy boy.

"Ten? And you still don't know how to read a simple list?"

"What's so bad about that? Lots of kids I know can't read."

"Well, I've been reading since I was five," said the boy, puffing out his chest with pride.

"Okay, so why don't you read it for me?" The scruffy boy retrieved the wrinkled paper and handed it over.

The lad's finger touched each word as he read it slowly, the scruffy boy looking over his shoulder. "Bone meal, potash, soda ash, lye, castile soap, vinegar. What the blazes kind of list is that?"

"Don't you know how to prepare the soil for corn plantin'?" The lad shook his head no. "Well, I been helpin' my daddy with the harvest since I was four. The first two things on that list help the soil, and the other things are needed to make a solution for killing weeds."

"Huh. I just eat it."

"Yeah, well, I hope you keep eatin' it, 'cause that's what puts food on our table." The scruffy boy smiled.

"You know how to play jacks?" asked the lad.

"Sure."

"C'mon. We can have a game while Papa has that clerk all occupied."

My friends, acceptance comes from the heart of a child rather than the eyes of man. Matthew writes, "I tell you the truth, unless you change and become like little children, you will

233

never enter the kingdom of heaven."

The Gospel writer also states, "But if anyone causes one of these little ones who believe in me to sin, it would be better for him to have a large millstone hung around his neck and to be drowned in the depths of the sea."

When deciding whether or not you have analyzed scripture correctly, ask yourself if your interpretations are rooted in the Golden Rule and believed with a child's humility and understanding.

He folded the paper from which he read and added, "You can start here, from Proverbs 30:8, 'Remove far from me falsehood and lying; give me neither poverty nor riches; feed me with the food that is needful for me.'" He winked at the congregation and repeated "feed me with the food that is needful for me." And after a dramatic pause, he concluded, "Interpret this line, defend it, and I will be at your side."

And he was. At the next demonstration, Father Laurence walked with us, and he continued to use his pulpit to preach to the common man. On one occasion, his homily brought the reverent church, always silent and solemn in their worship, to an exploding applause followed by a standing ovation and even a few hoots and hollers. The monsignor, unfortunately, was incensed and transferred our dear priest not only to a different parish, but a different diocese in a different state. Father Laurence was added to my list of intentions.

CHAPTER 35

Dieter's Tailor Shop was a small business located in the center of five narrow row house buildings, and it shared its brick walls with a storefront bakery to the east and a shoe shop to the west. Each establishment had a front bay with a large panel of glass in the center and a single-hung window on each side. Whenever I opened the shop, the first thing I did was lift the window facing east, no matter the weather, and then open the door that separated the customer counter from the work room. By leaving the back door ajar, a cross breeze would carry the sweet aroma of sugar and bread and tangy fruits to my sewing table. Sometimes, depending on the wind's strength and direction, the smells of leather and polish and glue made their way around the bay to create a unique mixture of scents, not bad or irritating to my sinuses, but a strange combination of feminine and masculine fragrances. Either way, the absence of smog odors was appreciated each working day, even if it was only for a couple of hours.

I was adjusting the buttons on a gray wool jacket when I heard the bell jingle. Dieter called out from his office next to my room that he'd be with the customers momentarily, to which the women replied in unison, "Take your time." They brought with them the aroma of fresh baked strawberry tarts with hints of cinnamon and saddle soap.

"He's a brute, Clara. Always has been, even when he was a newcomer on the force."

"Do you remember him and his friend, what was his name?

The other first year policeman with the same ego? The two of them used to bully anyone who stepped in front of them."

"Faust, wasn't it?" The buttons from my hand fell to the floor. "Rolf Faust. Yes, I remember it clearly now, Rolf Faust." I rose from my chair and stood against the wall beside the doorway.

"That's it, Agnes," Clara said to her friend. "Bonfield and Faust. What a team they were, acting high and mighty in their uniforms as they paraded themselves down the street. They thought they were above the law back then, and Bonfield thinks it's still the same."

Agnes agreed. "At least Faust's been gone a long time. That one was a bad seed, I'd say, even worse than old Bonfield, if you ask me."

"Didn't he target your brother for something?"

"He sure did. Bonfield and Faust raided a drinking party, and my brother Jimmy handed over the stuff, but Faust decided he wanted Jimmy's money, too, and Jimmy wouldn't give it to him. So that Faust beat him pretty bad, and Bonfield just watched and laughed. They ended up taking the money and Jimmy's hat and jacket to boot." I could picture Agnes shaking her head in disbelief of the memory.

Dieter approached the counter and gingerly set the skirts and jackets in a pile.

"And what's all this violent talk, here, ladies?"

"Just rememberin' the time when Bonfield was new to the force. He seems to get meaner with every promotion, and now that he's captain, he's rulin' the roost and using some harsh antics these days."

"That, he is, Agnes. It's a shame, too. He might be a rotten apple, but the whole force is not that way. He gives our policemen a bad name," Dieter replied.

"Were you around in the 50s when Faust was alive?" Clara asked.

"I sure was. And it was a blessing when he was killed."

A slight gasp escaped my mouth, but the patrons didn't seem to hear.

She went on, "The only sorrow in that death was his crazy wife and hoodlum child being left to fend for themselves."

"What ever happened to them?" Clara questioned.

"Within a couple of years, the boy ran away and the wife went to the asylum. Of course, the delinquent returned only to find that his mama was already dead and buried. If Bonfield hadn't taken that boy under his wing, he would've spent his life in prison."

"Well, it's probably where he belonged," said Clara.

"Bonfield let that boy do as he pleased, no matter how serious the crime. And God forgive me, but when he was drafted into the army, I was hoping he'd be put on the front lines, not on some kind of hospital desk duty. How do you like that? The lunatic files medical records while all the good boys are being blown to pieces."

One side appeared to be a blank prescription form, but the other side had writing... Karl Faust - to whom you owe your life...

"Well, ladies, I urge you to think of happier thoughts than

237

Bonfield and Faust. It's a beautiful day, and you should enjoy it. I, on the other hand, have to get back to work." Dieter handed the clothes to each customer. "I presume I'll add this to your accounts like before?"

"Yes, Dieter, thank you." And the ladies walked out, picking up on their conversation as soon as they left. The jingle from the overhead door frame quieted to a tinny silence, and my mind could not help but dwell on the discussion of a man named Rolf Faust. I wanted to know more. For the first time I thought about questioning Mrs. Heinrich, the only trusted person in my world who would have details about the bully of a man from years ago.

I waited until we were alone, after Tilly was asleep and the nighttime chores complete.

"Could you come to my room, Mrs. Heinrich, where I could talk with you discreetly?" I asked. "I'm a bit frazzled by a discussion I overheard at the tailor shop today, and I was wondering if you could shed some light on the topic."

My bedroom was still as bare as when we first moved in with a simple bed and single dresser. The wooden floors and hollow walls remained naked, allowing voices to echo when spoken above a whisper; even then, if someone wanted to hear my prayerful pleas, it wouldn't take more than an ear to the door. My elder friend obliged the request, and I motioned for her to sit beside me on the mattress. I brought up Rolf Faust's name, and Mrs. Heinrich's face went pale, an almost identical response to mine when Junior first spoke of meeting Karl at the newsstand.

"Where did you hear that name?" she inquired, inching closer to the edge of the bed, back straight and chin tilted upward, as one would sit during cross examination for a crime he didn't commit.

Her mannerisms alone told me that she had not only heard the name, but she personally knew the cold-hearted man described at Dieter's. I explained the conversation I overheard.

"He was the devil," she said, now gazing at the maple planks beneath our feet, but I could see the pain in her expression, and I didn't feel comfortable pressing the matter. However, Mrs. Heinrich seemed willing to elaborate. "He had an ego the size of a house, that man, and when a name got on his target list, there was nowhere to hide. Anyone who betrayed him, or questioned him, or stood up against him, anyone could be at his mercy, and that's the way he wanted it. Sometimes he took matters into his own hands, and other times he'd pay off a homeless bum to do the dirty work for him. And that helpless bum would end up getting caught and hung for crimes he committed on Rolf's behalf. He was a no good man, Livia, but you need to know something else." She stopped. She looked at me straight in the eye and took a deep breath. "Your Uncle George was one of his victims."

I knew it.

"Did you know Uncle George personally, Mrs. Heinrich?" I asked.

"I did."

"Did my parents know that you were acquainted?"

"When I was first introduced to your mother, Livia, I only

knew her by her first name. She was simply Johanna. Our shifts were always changing, and even when we worked together, your mother was on the quiet side. I knew her to be kind, from the moment she came to help when my husband had his accident. That was many years ago." Mrs. Heinrich paused, maybe reflecting on a memory of her spouse. She took a deep breath and straightened her back again. With hands picking lint off her skirt, she went on. "But a while into our acquaintance, she referred to Otto Haas, her husband. My jaw dropped, and I didn't know what to say, if it was even possible this Otto could be the brother of George to whom he referred so often."

"So you and Uncle George were close?"

"Close? I adored George. Neither of us grew up in these parts. Neither of us had any family in Chicago, and we didn't know many people, either. We met at a picnic. I attended with a couple of girls who stayed in the same boarding house as me. George was there with a few workers from the tobacco factory. Bonfield and Faust were up to their old tricks, harassing everyone. I decided to go for a short walk, and Faust caught my arm. He made advances toward me which I fought, but he was very strong. He told me that if I yelled, it would be the last time my voice would be heard." Mrs. Heinrich's gaze turned hypnotic, her eyes looking out through a protective film. Tilting her head as if she was observing someone or something just beyond my shoulder, she continued in a quiet voice, above a whisper but only slightly. "I was so afraid, Livia," she said, "but then a stranger, your uncle, came up to us, and without any fear he told Faust to let me go before he ripped the badge off his

240

chest and gathered an all-too happy mob to whip him. Needless to say, that event sparked many things. George and I became an item, Faust put George on his target list, and for the next three months, our lives were in danger with every passing day."

"Oh, Mrs. Heinrich," I gasped. "What a coincidence that you would become friends with our family."

"Not a coincidence, Livia." This time she peered directly into my eyes. "I don't believe in coincidences. Divine intervention, maybe, or George watching over us from the other side, but it was no coincidence when your mother mentioned her husband, Otto Haas. It was just after the fire, when the sewing circle was starting to regroup, and I needed to know if Johanna was related to George. We were working the same day-shift that time, so while we walked home, I asked her about Otto's family. We talked for hours, and I shared with her my story, and then Otto joined us. He wanted to know how George died and where he was buried. I told him everything, and later that week I took your parents to the little cemetery on the land of the asylum."

"Can you tell me how they died? Rolf and Uncle George."

Her eyes went searching again, to that spot beyond my shoulder, to a time from long ago.

"The Lager Beer Riots took place in '55. It was pure chaos, and while the protesters were still on the bridge, Rolf decided to start raising it, to put an end to the riot and hopefully put an end to the lives of the men who were stuck. Of course, George was one of the men, and when he fell he was trampled by people and the police horses. He lost his right leg, but he survived the riot. I was concerned about him. He lost his job at the tobacco factory because he was maimed; soon, an infection set in. Faust was hunting him down."

Mrs. Heinrich touched her throat.

"Do you need a drink of water?" I asked. She nodded, and I obliged.

"Thank you, Livia. I can continue." She took a strong inhale and picked up where she left off. "After work one day, I went to his boarding house to check on him, to bring him some soup and see if there was anything else I could do. But when I got there, I noticed a group of tenants gathered on the front lawn, and they told me not to go inside, that Faust threatened them and told them that if anyone entered the house, they'd be arrested for disobedience. I ran to George's room anyway and found Rolf beating your poor uncle." Mrs. Heinrich pleaded with me, as if she was trying to make a case, "He only had one leg! He couldn't stand; he couldn't defend himself!" Her hands went to her heart. "George's screams of help were unanswered because no one was there to assist him. My mind went blank, and without thinking it through, without thinking about the consequences, I took George's pistol from the bureau—"

Mrs. Heinrich trembled and held out her hands as if an invisible gun was there, as if she was back at the boarding house and aiming at Rolf Faust's head.

"I shot him." She sighed. "I shot him."

She dropped her imaginary weapon and let her back arch over. She brought her fingers to her face and sobbed lightly. I sat closer and pulled her body against mine. "It's okay," I kept repeating, "it's okay."

"George was barely alive himself from the brutal beating. He thanked me for saving him and for loving him; he said he loved me, too and that I needed to give him the gun and run to save myself."

I handed her a handkerchief, and she composed herself.

"One of the boarders had followed me inside and took me away from the scene; I was gone before the police arrived. I was told that George was taken to the Dunning asylum and died the next day. Lord knows what kind of torture he endured. I don't know what it was like back then, but when I took your parents about twenty years later, to Dunning, it was just awful. Had I known what a terrible place it was with its wooden structures packed with cots where crazed men and women, stench and disease, ran rampant, I would not have allowed Otto and Johanna to come. We asked the office worker where, exactly, George was buried on their land, which of the three cemeteries he was in. The worker walked us outside and pointed west at a large clearing. He said that if George died in the 50s, his body was most likely exhumed from where we were standing and moved over there, but if he was an orphan or civil war veteran or fire victim, he'd be in the clearing further south. Matter-of-factly he spoke, as if there was nothing wrong with how the living were treated and how the dead were buried. It made me sick inside, but for your mother, she got violently ill. She couldn't handle the place, and I wouldn't be surprised if the memory of that day didn't haunt her."

They will take him! Hurry! Save him! No morgue! He has a name! Tell them his name!

"The boarder that protected me was Henri Heinrich. He was one of the few real friends that George had. We married quickly for no other reason than to protect me in case someone connected me to George or to the crime. But no one questioned me. The police pegged George for the murder all along."

"Thank you, Mrs. Heinrich, for being there for him," I said.

"Don't thank me, Livia. It was a terrible sin, a sin for which I must repent every day of my life, but I praise the Lord for granting me the opportunity to share my guilt with you. This was a sin that Mrs. Faust couldn't cope with. The woman was mad in the first place, but after Rolf's death, she became a lunatic, so insane that in several years' time she, too, was sent to the asylum, and that hellion of a son was left on his own."

I took a deep breath.

"Do you remember the son's name to be Karl?"

"Yes, dear. Karl Faust, the one who got his hands on Franz's records which brought him into your lives."

"So, my parents told you about him, then?"

"They did. And I'll tell you the same I told them. Without any question in my mind, that devil drugged Franz. He had access to all those pills in the medical tents. He made sure Franz would talk and never remember a thing."

"When Franz spoke of Jonas, I bet it made Karl's heart race because of the similarities between him and Uncle George. Karl told me he wanted Jonas, but God took care of him first."

Mrs. Heinrich placed a soothing hand on top of my head.

"I guess that might have been divine intervention, too. I hate to think of the torture Karl would have inflicted on Jonas, had

244

Jonas not died of typhoid." She smoothed a wisp of hair away from my face and over my ear. "Karl delighted in seeing our family in pain."

"Your parents also told me about what happened during the fire, Livia. I know what Karl did to you."

"Their answer was for me to marry Franz."

"Franz was safe," she explained. "He wasn't rebellious like Jonas and George, so you had a better chance of Karl leaving you alone."

"You mean, he wasn't an agitator."

"Exactly."

She hugged me, and as I cried, Mrs. Heinrich rocked and spoke to me. "I'm sorry we had to keep this a secret, but your parents were protecting me with their silence. I don't care about the consequences anymore, but back then there was too much at stake with Henri."

I took her hands in mine. "Mother and Father were right to keep quiet, Mrs. Heinrich, and the details need not be told again."

"Is there something you want to tell me, Livia?" she asked. "A story of your own, maybe?"

For the first time, I bared my soul and shared with Mrs. Heinrich my own agitator's story, my story of Will Magee.

CHAPTER 36

"We're getting married!"

Junior's eyes were locked on Mary's as he made the announcement at suppertime.

"Oh my goodness!" I exclaimed. "What news!"

Tilly jumped out of her chair and clapped in joyous response. Mrs. Heinrich made a sign of the cross and clasped her hands on the table. I rose with my arms outstretched.

"I can't describe my elation," Mary said, and she came to me for a tight embrace. "We are going to be so happy."

There was nothing I wanted more than for that to be true. "Of course, you are, sweetie."

Junior stood straight and proud, waiting his turn for a hug, and when Mary let go and stepped aside, we froze and looked at one another in silence. No words were necessary to express all that we two had endured and how much well-deserved happiness this wedding would bring to our family. He took me in his arms and let my head rest on his chest.

"Father Laurence will be in town next week," he whispered, "and he has agreed to officiate."

Our arms remained wrapped, but I tilted my head up to speak. "Next week?"

"We don't want to wait. We love each other, Liv. Do you approve of this?"

"Do I approve?" I giggled. "I more than approve, Junior." My fingers touched his cheeks. "And I'm honored to represent your parents' blessing. Franz and Catherine are both smiling on this moment." He smiled.

"May I ask you two questions?"

"Certainly."

Junior turned his touch to Mary, putting an arm around her shoulder and posing his first request on their behalf.

"We were wondering if you'd allow us to be married here, in the parlor. It would be a simple service, of course, with just us and Mary's parents."

Mrs. Heinrich and Tilly noticed the unconscious once-over my eyes made, as they replied for me. "How wonderful!" and "We will surely help with the preparations."

"Mrs. Dietz?" asked Mary.

"Oh, Mary, yes. By all means I want you to have your wedding here!"

"Thank you. It will be beautiful."

"What will you wear?" cried an excited Tilly.

"Well," replied Junior, "that's the second question. What do you think of Mary wearing my mother's dress, the one in the cedar chest?"

I envisioned Mary's shoulders setting the flow of the gown, her neckline perfectly fashioned for the delicate v-shaped top.

"Absolutely."

Later that night, I sat in the kitchen with Catherine's treasured garment, and I removed the lavender ribbon from the amber wheat lace. Thread by thread, I recalled the memories and hope the dress had brought to the women who wore it, as well as the men who touched it. I rolled the ribbon into a ball and placed it in my apron pocket next to my worry stone.

Junior and Mary shared their special event with a national event in the labor movement. They requested the day off at the lumber yards and sewing factory but did not get a response from their employers; therefore, the couple never showed up for work on May 1. However, thousands of others across the country clocked in and then walked off their jobs that day. When everyone else in Chicago set down their tools and turned off their machines, Father Laurence set down his Bible on my parlor table and turned toward the young man and woman before him.

"We are gathered here today—"

(Signaling church bells rang in the distance.)

"Will you marry me, Livia Haas?"

"Do you promise to love one another in sickness and in health?"

(Feet scampered across floors toward doors that opened to the promise of a new day.)

"I pledge to you and to God to love and honor you, Liv, to do what's right by you. I do."

"Let us celebrate."

(Demonstrations flooded the streets.)

He lifted me into his arms and cradled me against his chest, escorting me this way to the back room and gently setting me on a cushioned chaise.

CHAPTER 37

Junior arranged to be at a rally on Monday morning for the lumber union strikers, and I planned to follow my usual routine – tailor shop, paper office, home. Plans changed quickly when word spread that a tragic attack was taking place at the McCormick Reaper Works. I hadn't contemplated going anywhere near the supposed battle, until I was told that many lumber strikers had joined the McCormick strikers. Visions of police guns being aimed in Junior's direction, visions of Mrs. Heinrich aiming at Rolf Faust, caused me to flee immediately.

When I arrived, I was told by a bystander that blood had already been shed with Bonfield having led his troops through the strikers, killing two men and wounding countless others, even women and children and local residents who just happened to be at the wrong place at the wrong time. I searched for Junior, and while pushing my way through a group, I was cuffed, shoved into a wagon and brought to the station with others.

The jail was insufferable, filthy and dark, smelling worse than anything I had ever smelled in my life. Sweaty men yelled and cursed from behind metal bars as I was escorted down a dingy hallway, my head aching with pin-like pain around my eyes, and that's when it happened —I noticed him. At least I thought I noticed him. *Will*! The figure had Will's body, and he was looking down at his cuffed wrists with hands which were holding a necklace of some kind—no, not a necklace—beads! The man was holding and praying a rosary!

"Will!" I screamed out, and as soon as the man lifted his

head in my direction, the guards ushered him around the corner and whisked me into a cage with ten other women. I sat anxiously with the image of Will and the possibility of Karl stepping into the room, of Junior being held in another cell with Will walking by him, too. I tried praying, but I couldn't focus with the constant noise and odor around me.

The keys rattled in the lock, startling me as the door sprang open. Another female outlaw was foisted into the already crowded space when I looked up at her with reddened cheeks. Watery lashes blurred my sight, but I saw her dark-caramel complexion and her feisty movements and confident airs. Our eyes locked.

"Sweet Jesus, you're alive!" she exclaimed.

"Clem?"

She ran up to me and took my face in her hands; her nimble fingers pressed against my ears like she was checking a melon for ripeness.

"Sweet Jesus, you *are* alive!" she repeated, and our arms wrapped around one another. "I didn't believe him when he told me. I wanted to finds ya and see for myself, and here you are!" She lifted her arms in the air. "Praise, Jesus! Here you are!"

"Oh, Clem. I've prayed for you, my friend. For you and Will, every day."

"Did ya sees him?" she asked.

"Will's back from Wisconsin, isn't he? He's here."

Clem nodded.

I felt lightheaded, and the throbbing intensified, pulsing hard at the temples and into the jaw. I was speechless and dropped onto a bench to catch my breath.

"Girl, you tremblin' like a leaf."

"I just saw him, Clem."

"Clementine Barnett!" the guard called. "There's some kind of lawyer here, sayin' he's related to you. Let's go!"

"That's my cousin comin' to get me. I'll see Will sometime next week, after all this lumber strikin' settles down," Clementine started.

"Barnett, NOW!"

"I promise to tell him I saw you, Liv. Where can he find ya?"

The guard stepped up and grabbed her by the arm, but she didn't take her eyes off me.

"Dieter's tailor shop on—" I started to explain, and she was gone.

I sat motionless for a minute or ten hours, until Junior found me and took me home.

CHAPTER 38

Lord knows what time it was. All the room was black as pitch, and the pillow was wet with perspiration, yet I was cold, goosebumps running from toe to finger, as I blindly searched for the blanket that had been kicked to the floor. His face was clear as day in my head. Wrapping myself in the crocheted knit, I snugged tightly, trying to hold my body in place and forcing my limbs to remain still.

The morning arrived like a train wreck, crashing through my window, demanding evacuation from twisted rails of anxiety that came to an abrupt yet temporary halt, and I knew it wouldn't take much to make my mind explode. I moved through the morning and afternoon, still picturing the prison cell, not remembering if I had had my cup of tea or left the water boiling in the kitchen, whether I had mended collars or buttons or hems, how Tilly's day had gone. Somehow the evening hours were upon me again, but I couldn't stop the wheels of thoughts in my head, rolling on and on—Uncle George's letters, Karl's twitching and glaring eyes, Will's smile and words— *won't I forever encourage the questioning of mere men.*

Mary peeked in on me.

"Junior told Otelia he would have a checkers competition with her tonight," said Mary. "Sarah and I thought we'd attend the sewing girls' meeting."

"Is that this evening?" I asked, not looking in her direction. "The one with the A.G.I. representatives?"

"That's the one. Would you like to join us?"

The American Group of the International was an organization with which Lucy and Lizzie were affiliated, and they planned the gathering to brainstorm an agenda for the sewing girls, still in desperate need of workplace reform. The offer to attend the gathering seemed like an opportune escape from my wandering brain. I stood and said I would go.

The hall was crowded with mingling skirts, some heads held high while others dropped for anonymity, and the air dense with a wall of humidity. The meeting was called to order just minutes after we arrived, and a straightforward agenda was announced. Lucy never stopped speaking when she noticed me, giving me a nod of recognition and a smile of gratitude. The girls and I volunteered once again to post and distribute circulars, while other responsibilities were promptly delegated. Lizzie motioned for me to come over to her table. Little Lulu and Albert Jr. sat yawning, and Lucy stood nearby in conversation with three representatives, when a messenger entered the front doors and scurried his way to the Parsons family. He directed his request to Albert Sr. and his friend Mr. Fielden standing only a few feet away.

"Mr. Parsons, sir, Mr. Spies says that your immediate presence is needed at the meeting at Haymarket Square."

"I already said I had plans. Aren't there other speakers?" asked Albert.

"No, sir. Mr. Spies is the only one. He has already addressed the crowd about the atrocities that took place at McCormick's yesterday, but he needs another orator and sent me to give you and Mr. Fielden this request."

Albert turned to Lucy who had been listening to the plea.

"We're finished here, anyway, Albert."

"You can tell Mr. Spies that we're on our way," he said to the messenger.

"Thank you, sir." And he ran out the door.

When the Parsons, Lizzie, and the Fieldens left, the sewing girls met in small groups to access their duties. It was late, but some workers who had witnessed the assaults at the Reaper Works decided to head over to Haymarket to hear what the speakers might have to say. Privately, I couldn't help but wonder if Will might be there, too.

Mary went home, but Sarah and I joined several girls in walking over to the gathering on Randolph Street near DesPlaines Avenue. By the time we approached the speakers' wagon, Spies and the Parsons family were already gone. Everything was coming to a close with Mr. Fielden making his last remarks.

"Have a good evening, Mr. Mayor," said Sarah.

Mayor Carter Harrison, keeping a casual pace as he strolled down the street, tipped his brown fedora at my young friend, his unruly whiskers parting between mustache and beard to show a simple smile. When he passed us, we heard him tell the gentleman next to him that all was fine, that he was heading home.

The weather threatened to turn sour with a drizzle tickling the bodies of the now modest crowd, so we planned on leaving when Sarah's facial expression turned from a grin to a frustrated frown .

"Well, isn't that unnecessary," Sarah stated.

"Unnecessary?" I asked.

"That." She pointed toward the alley opening and street corners, where I spotted the line of horses being ridden in what appeared to be a well coordinated approach. More lines of National Guardsmen moved forward from every direction, clubs at the ready being held in one hand and pounded into the palm of the other like drumbeats growing in rhythm and volume. It didn't take long for the first verbal combat to begin between Bonfield's warriors and the labor movement followers. Slurs and curses were thrown through the air while fists were threatening to connect. Pure chaos would surely ensue, and I froze at the senselessness of it all.

"Let's get out of here," said Sarah, and she grabbed hold of my sleeve, pulling me toward the walkway.

"Livia!"

I jolted. I heard it, my name, plain as day, being called by a voice so dear. "Livia!" it cried out again, and I searched the mass of faces, my eyes darting in every direction, concentrating on my name, when an image came through the stampede of uniformed men like the parting of the Red Sea, and I saw him pushing his way toward me. I was desperate to reach out to him, to touch him, to hold him!

"Will!"

"LIVIA HAAS!" This time the call came from another direction, from somewhere behind me, where the lines were closing in, and I knew that voice, too. Cold fear stopped me in my tracks. Will was in sight in front of me, and he was moving nearer and nearer, but I turned around when I heard that guttural call again, "LIVIA HAAS!" Karl was in laborer clothes with one hand in his coat, reaching—reaching for something that looked like a stick. Will yelled out again, and my head swung back to him in earnest, but his hands frantically motioned for me to *GET AWAY!*

"WILL!" I screamed simultaneously with, and being drowned out by, the mighty BOOM! With the explosion, sparks flew and smoke enveloped the crowd; people dropped to the ground. Shots rang out, and clubs started pounding down on heads and backs and legs, and all hell surrounded me. I ran to where Will fell, and I held him to me, blood dripping from his body onto mine.

"Dear God, no!" I cried, lifting his body slightly, so I could sit behind and cradle him. I rocked him, begging for the Lord's mercy.

"Livia, 'tis really you," he said quietly, attempting a smile, his eyes still twinkling.

He coughed, and I held him closer as a bewildered and disheveled man came to our side.

"Naw, Will, naw. This can't be happenin'. Stay still while I tie up this here leg, eh," and the man took off his jacket and tied it around Will's thigh. "I'm goin' to get help. Ya hear me, Will? Hang on, man, and Miss," he looked up at me, "won't ya watch over me brother-in-law."

I nodded, unable to speak after taking notice of Will's leg losing blood.

"Stay strong, Will. Please stay strong," I implored. I heard him whimper as he reached into his pocket and pulled out a book wrapped in beads.

The journal slipped from his hand and fell to his side. I took it.

"Wasn't I supposed to be the one to pick it up, eh?"

"You can't leave me again, Will. You can't."

"The Lord works in mysterious ways, indeed." He took a deep breath. "If not in this lifetime, we'll be meetin' again someday. I love ya, Livia Haas, I do." I grabbed Will's hand, and he gave it a squeeze.

PROCLAMATION TO THE PEOPLE OF CHICAGO
MAYOR'S OFFICE, Chicago, May 5, 1886

WHEREAS, great excitement exists among the people of this good city, growing out of the LABOR TROUBLES, which excitement is intensified by the open defiance of the guardians of the peace by a body of lawless men, who, under the pretense of aiding the laboring men, are really endeavoring to destroy all law. And whereas, last night these men, by the use of weapons never resorted to in CIVILIZED LANDS. EXCEPT IN TIMES OF WAR or for REVOLUTIONARY PURPOSES, CAUSED GREAT BLOODSHED AMOND CITIZENS AND AMONG OFFICERS of the MUNICIPALITY who were simply in the performance of their duties. And Whereas, the CITY AUTHORITIES PROPOSE TO PROTECT LIFE AND PROPERTY AT ALL HAZARDS, and in doing so will be compelled to break up all unlawful or dangerous gatherings; and

WHEREAS, Even when men propose to meet for lawful purposes, bad men will attempt to mingle with them, armed with cowardly missiles, for the purpose of bringing about bloodshed, thus endangering innocent persons:

THEREFORE, I, Carter H. Harrison, MAYOR OF THE CITY OF CHICAGO, DO HEREBY PROCLAIM THAT GATHERINGS OF PEOPLE IN CROWDS OR PROCESSIONS IN THE STREETS and PUBLIC PLACES OF THE CITY ARE DANGEROUS AND CANNOT BE PERMITTED, AND ORDERS HAVE BEEN ISSUED TO THE POLICE TO PREVENT ALL SUCH GATHERINGS and TO BREAK UP and DISPERSE ALL CROWDS, TO PREVENT INJURY TO INNOCENT PERSONS.

I urge all law-abiding people to quietly attend to their own affairs, and not to meet in crowds. If the police order any gatherings to disperse, and they be no obeyed, all persons so disobeying, will be treated as law-breakers, and will surely incur the penalty of their disobedience.

I further assure the good people of Chicago that I believe the police can protect their lives and property and the name of Chicago, and WILL do so.

CARTER H. HARRISON, Mayor

"I appeal not for mercy, but for justice. As for me, the utterance of Patrick Henry is so apropos that I cannot do better than let him speak: 'Is life so dear and peace so sweet as to be purchased at the price of chains and slavery? Forbid it, Almighty God! I know not what course others may pursue, but as for me, give me liberty or give me death!'" - Albert Parsons, September 21, 1887

THE ANARCHISTS' FATE

Executed on November 11, 1887:
Albert Parsons, August Spies, George Engel, Adolph Fischer
Death by suicide while imprisoned:
Louis Lingg
Sentenced to fifteen years of hard labor:
Oscar Neebe
Sentenced to life imprisonment:
Michael Schwab, Samuel Fielden

Love -- is anterior to Life --
Posterior -- to Death --
Initial of Creation, and
The Exponent of Earth --

(Emily Dickinson)

CHAPTER 39

"I want to open another tobacco store," Junior announced one day. I was hesitant, but Junior was intelligent and vibrant and the model of determination. His passion for this venture was evident, so I told him I would support his goals and work for him.

"I have a different plan for you, Liv. I'll take care of the tobacco business, while you go to university and get your degree."

"What?"

"You heard me right, Liv. I've saved enough money to open the shop and pay your tuition. I want you to get that degree."

Tilly was enthusiastic, pleading with me to get started on my education, not just for myself, but to set precedence for other women who had been deprived such opportunities.

"You've always been supportive of my independent thought," she told me. "A truer role model I could never ask for." My daughter took my hands in hers. "Please, Mother, do this for me," she implored.

I agreed to apply. If accepted, I would go to school part-time and work for Junior part-time, and I would not take a single penny's worth of wages until the diploma was in my hand.

By June 1893, my education degree was hanging on our wall. By June 1893, the World's Columbian Exposition was attracting people worldwide to Chicago. By June 1893, a Haymarket memorial was scheduled for dedication.

"You're sure you want to go alone?" Tilly asked.

"I feel I must," I replied.

"We'll meet after Junior's shift at the fair?"

"That's the plan," I smiled.

Tilly straightened the ribbon around my neck. "It's a special day," she said. "You look divine."

I watched my daughter from the parlor window as she bounced down the stairs and headed toward the street. She stopped and looked up at the tree in our front yard. Smiling, she knelt to the ground and picked up an acorn that had fallen. She kissed it and put it in her pocket before continuing her walk.

At the train station I joined hundreds of citizens waiting to head west to Forest Park. When we arrived, the murmur of the crowd grew and quieted like a wave of cicada sounds as we gathered just inside the main entrance at Waldheim Cemetery. We moved in unison down the paved lane, swerving gently to the south to their place of rest. A calm and scenic place, the structure, hidden by a tarp, was the backdrop for the speakers when they, one by one, shared words of praise for the activists who sacrificed their lives for the cause of the eight hour day; "the Haymarket martyrs" they were called. An excerpt from Governor John Altgeld's pardon would soon read:

"These charges are of a personal character, and while they seem to be sustained by the record of the trial and the papers before me and tend to show that the trial was not fair, I do not care to discuss this feature of the case any farther, because it is not necessary. I am convinced that it is clearly my duty to act in this case for the reasons already given, and I, therefore, grant an absolute pardon to Samuel Fielden, Oscar Neebe, and Michael Schwab this 26th day of June, 1893."

The applause was deafening when Lucy stood to address the crowd. She had aged, as did we all, but the spark was still in her eye. Her crusade to clear her husband's name, to bring equality in pay and safety in working conditions, to ensure fairness in workday hours—all of the fight was still erupting from her lips as she spoke, and the listeners cheered her on. Next, Albert Jr. drew back the heavy cloth, unveiling the Haymarket memorial. A brief moment of silence was given in respect for those whose lives were sacrificed. The monument was comprised of two bronze figures; a woman of justice and a fallen laborer. "Justice" was preparing to draw her sword with her right hand, while her left hand was placing a crown of laurels on the worker's head. After studying the work of art, it dawned on me why I was connected to the laborer's depiction: his hair had wavy locks, similar to those of Jonas. My brother would have liked that. The compelling image was enhanced with an inscription of August Spies' last words: "The day will come when our silence will be more powerful than the voices you are throttling today."

After the ceremony, I made my way to the old neighborhood, to St. Michael Parish. Walking through the prominent wooden doors, the tabernacle seemed farther away than I remembered, and the aisle appeared like a never ending road. I sat down in a pew near the back and looked around at everything that had changed, and everything that still remained the same. I opened my bag, took out the journal, and unraveled the beads. I turned to the first page and read my words, "Do I smell all right?" *Everything turned out the way God planned, hadn't it?* I accepted it all. Embraced it all. How blessed I was to come to this moment in *life*, when so many of my loved ones could only find peace in death. It seemed important to pray for them and thank them for bringing me to this day. I was early. I had time to say a rosary.

Hail, Holy Queen, Mother of Mercy,
our life, our sweetness and our hope!

Bless you, Mother and Father, for instilling in me the importance of faith and devotion — "May Your will be done, and may we accept the path You intend."

To you we cry,
poor banished children of Eve;

Bless you, Uncle George, for giving the words that inspired my own —"they are simply too exhausted and poor to take part in its pulsing appeal."

to you we send up our sighs,
mourning and weeping in the valley of tears.

Bless you, Catherine, for modeling a sense of intellect and pride in oneself— "her gait was upright, and she was the only one of us to walk with a fully vertical stride."

Turn then, most gracious advocate,

your eyes of mercy toward us;

Bless you, little George, for showing me how to appreciate life, no matter the obstacle— "he teaches us every day to accept our hardships and appreciate our blessings."

and after this our exile,

show us to the blessed fruit of your womb, Jesus.

Bless you, Franz, for reminding me that I still had a moral center— "At some point, we must stop following rules and start following our hearts."

O clement, O loving,

O sweet Virgin Mary;

Bless you, Mrs. Heinrich, for teaching me how to accept imperfection with humility and grace— "It was a terrible sin, a sin for which I must repent every day of my life, but I praise the Lord for granting me the opportunity to share my guilt with you."

Pray for us,

O holy Mother of God.

Bless you, Jonas. So righteous were your beliefs that they guided me each time I stood up or marched on— "I lay my head each night with good conscience."

That we may be made worthy of the promises

of Christ.

The time had to be near. *His letter said 3:00, right?* I retrieved the paper from my bag to confirm the time:

"Although I was not classified an anarchist, I was given the same sentence, and hence, given the same pardon. Won't you meet me at St. Michael's at 3:00 and exchange vows with me, officially? I still want to do what's right by you, Livia. I want you to be my wife, right here, right now, in this lifetime, eh? I look forward to seeing my girl."

The side door opened and let the sun cascade onto the wooden planks, reflecting off the cross on the altar. The tapping of a cane blended with the rhythm of the footsteps. I couldn't contain the smile when I saw him. Leaving my belongings in the pew, I met him at the front of the church.

"You are more beautiful than ever," he said. Will placed his hands on my shoulders and let his thumbs rub the ribbon around my neck.

"I can't believe it's you, that you're here, that we're going to do this."

"Believe it, Livia. I'm not going anywhere without you."

The side door sounded again, and we turned toward it. "My family," I said. Junior entered first carrying his little Charlotte. Mary held hands with their son, Francis. My daughter walked in last with a bouquet of flowers. She handed them to me, and then the eyes of Will and Otelia met—the same smoky gray gaze.

"Here's your girl," I whispered. She was wearing a "Votes for Women" button.

ACKNOWLEDGEMENTS

The listed articles were found at the stated websites.

To Tramps:

Lucy E. Parsons, "To Tramps," Alarm, October 4, 1884. Also printed and distributed as a leaflet by the International Working People's Association.

http://courses.washington.edu/spcmu/speeches/lucyparsons.htm

Proclamation:

Chicago Historical Society - Haymarket Affair Digital Collection Proclamation to the people of Chicago: Mayor's office, May 5, 1886. Chicago (Ill.) Mayor. 1 broadside: 42 x 28 in. Chicago, Ill.: Jno. B. Jeffrey Printing & Engraving Co., 1886. (CHS ICHi 31325)

http://www.chicagohistory.org/hadc/visuals/05V0660.htm

Pardon:

The Pardon of the Haymarket Prisoners (June 26, 1893)

http://www.law2.umkc.edu/faculty/projects/ftrials/haymarket/pardon.html#REASONS_FOR_PARDONING

Words can't express my gratitude for those who voluntarily took time out to read and critique during various stages of my writing: Mom, Bob, Lorie, Mary W., Russ, Mindy, Debbie, Theresa, Nell, Peggy, Laurie, Kathy, Jerry, and Mary O.

Special thanks to Pat and the boys for respecting my novel time.

Special thanks to all the folks at the Friendly Lounge for offering a creative writing place with a passion for the arts.

Special thanks to every friend and student who encouraged me to keep at it!

Special thanks to the Chicago Writers Association and the Writer's Digest community for their wealth of inspiration and resources.

Here's the lesson I hope to have shared with my sons:
Don't ever give up on a dream! I love you, Ethan & Liam!